ALSO BY E. D. BAKER

The Fairy → Tale
MATCHMAKER

THE MAGICAL MATCH

E.D. BAKER

BLOOMSBURY

NEW YORK LONDON OXFORD NEW DELHI SYDNEY

First published in the United States of America in October 2017
by Bloomsbury Children's Books
www.bloomsbury.com

Bloomsbury is a registered trademark of Bloomsbury Publishing Plc

For information about permission to reproduce selections from this book, write to
Permissions, Bloomsbury Children's Books, 1385 Broadway, New York, New York 10018
Bloomsbury books may be purchased for business or promotional use. For information on
bulk purchases please contact Macmillan Corporate and Premium Sales Department at
specialmarkets@macmillan.com

Library of Congress Cataloging-in-Publication Data
available upon request
ISBN 978-1-68119-139-3 (hardcover) • ISBN 978-1-68119-140-9 (e-book)

Book design by Ellice Lee and John Candell
Typeset by Westchester Publishing Services
Printed and bound in the U.S.A. by Berryville Graphics Inc., Berryville, Virginia
2 4 6 8 10 9 7 5 3 1

All papers used by Bloomsbury Publishing, Inc., are natural, recyclable products
made from wood grown in well-managed forests. The manufacturing processes
conform to the environmental regulations of the country of origin.

I'd like to dedicate this book to Kim, my research assistant and sounding board, to Ellie, my trouble-shooter, to Kevin, my tech guru, to Victoria, one of the best teachers I've ever had, and to my fans, whose enthusiasm keeps me going.

≫→

CHAPTER
1

*C*ory shoved the letter through the mail slot in the door, rapped the door knocker three times, and ran to hide in the shrubs. Greener Pastures, the retirement community, was old-fashioned, although the residents called it quaint. No one there had message baskets the way they did in the big cities like New Town. Instead they relied on a letter carrier to go from house to house. There was only one letter carrier in Greener Pastures, so sometimes it took days or even weeks for a letter to reach its destination. Cory didn't have that kind of time. Besides, she was deliberately putting the letter in the slot at the wrong house, something a letter carrier would never do on purpose.

Cory sat down to watch the tree-stump house. Although it was only as big as her uncle Micah's garden shed, it was just the right size for a retired gnome living alone. If all went well, that situation was about to change.

Cory was the Cupid for the land of the fey. It was up to her to bring people together with their true loves. Her visions told her who belonged together. They were always right, but they didn't always come at convenient times.

Cory had taken over the job of Cupid from her grandfather only a few days before. The visions started coming thick and fast after that. Since that day, she had matched five sets of fairies, a pair of dwarves, and a human couple, all of whom lived in New Town. She'd had the vision of the two elderly gnomes for three days, but had been putting off the trip so she could handle the matches closer to home. When the visions started taking over her dreams, she knew it was the gnomes' turn.

The door opened and a man no taller than Cory's knee stepped out and looked around. He was holding Cory's envelope and he looked annoyed. "Gilbert Bean-worthy, you're the worst letter carrier ever!" he shouted, although there was no one but Cory to hear him. "You know my name isn't Mildred Treesap! This isn't even my address!"

The old gnome shut the door behind him and stomped down the path to the road to look both ways. When he didn't see anyone, he grunted and started walking.

"Darn centaurs!" he grumbled. "Don't know why they'd let one be a letter carrier anyway."

Cory crept through the underbrush, following the gnome at a distance. She moved as quietly as she could, although she doubted he could hear her over his own voice. When they reached an intersection, she darted across. He still didn't see her. It took almost ten minutes to reach the address on the envelope. The old gnome complained the entire way. He didn't stop even as he left the road and turned toward a house shaped like a giant mushroom. Cory thought the bright red mushroom with big white polka dots was pretty, but the old gnome started complaining about that, too.

"Must be rich, living in a mansion like this," he muttered. "Way too fancy if you ask me."

Cory was hiding behind the tall patch of decorative grass only a few yards from the door when the gnome started knocking. Less than a minute later, a white-haired lady gnome with a sweet face opened it. "Hello?" she said when she saw the grumpy-looking gnome.

"A letter for you was misdelivered to my house," he told her.

Cory was relieved to see both people from her vision standing face-to-face. Locating the two people who she was supposed to match, then getting them in the same place at the same time wasn't always easy. Her grandfather had suggested the wrong-address method, claiming it had often worked for him.

Bow! thought Cory, and her silver bow appeared in one hand, the quiver holding two arrows in the other. Time froze for everyone but Cory as she took out the first arrow. "Timothy Alfalfa Greengrass" was written on the shaft. She set the arrow even as she walked around for a better shot, then aimed it at the male gnome's heart. It hit with a soft *plunk* amid a shower of gold sparkles.

Turning toward the lady gnome, Cory took the other arrow from the quiver. "Mildred Springleaf Treesap" read the name. This time when the arrow hit its mark, the gold sparkles engulfed both gnomes. Cory was walking away when the sparkles faded and the two fell into each other's arms. She didn't glance back until she reached the road. When she saw their tender embrace, she smiled at a job well done.

Cory landed in the backyard of the house she now shared with her grandfather. With the powerful wings of a Cupid, she could fly higher and farther than she ever could as a fairy. As long as she could take off and land out of sight, she could fly on even the sunniest of days. Keeping secret the fact that she was Cupid was always on her mind. Everyone in her household knew, of course.

Even Macks, the ogre who had become her permanent bodyguard, knew that she was Cupid. Once she'd decided to employ him like the putti who had served her grandfather for years, she had told Macks the truth. To her surprise, he had been delighted and seemed to take great pride in working for her.

"Hey, Cory!" Macks called as she walked across the yard. "How'd it go?"

Shimmer, the copper-colored baby dragon, had been flying circles around Macks. Seeing Cory, she flew straight to her, landing in her arms. Cory laughed and petted the little dragon's head, saying, "It went very well. Did anything unusual happen here?"

Macks scratched his jaw and looked thoughtful. "I don't know if I'd call it unusual, seeing that we've had so many unwanted visitors, but Shimmer and I had to chase off two more flower fairies trying to plant poison ivy in the garden."

Although the courts had ruled against the guilds that had been persecuting Cory, angry guild members were still trying to make her life miserable. It was one of the reasons Cory had decided to make Macks's job permanent. The other reason was that everyone in the household liked him and didn't want to see him go. Even the putti had asked her if he could stay.

"Thank you, Macks," said Cory. "They can't get away with much of anything with you and Shimmer patrolling the grounds. Excuse me, you two. Sarilee is already looking for me. I don't know how she knows I'm back already."

The little putti woman was standing on the back terrace with a sheaf of leaves in her hand, waiting for Cory. Without being asked, she had started acting as Cory's assistant the morning after the position of Cupid had passed from grandfather to granddaughter. Cory sometimes thought the putti woman was a little too efficient.

"I need your reports before you do anything else," Sarilee told her. "You have to do the one for this morning and two for the matches you did last night. You really should fill them out while the names are still fresh in your mind. How did the match go today?"

"Very well," Cory said as she reached down to take the leaves from the putti. "The trick with the wrong address worked perfectly."

Sarilee nodded. "That was always one of your grandfather's favorites. We received a reply from your uncle, Micah. He and Quince will be happy to join you for supper tonight."

"Thanks," Cory said as she started into the house. "I'll be in my office if anything comes up."

She passed three more putti on the way to the room she'd claimed as her office. They all grinned and waved as she walked by. Cory had agreed to keep her grandfather's helpers and was already growing fond of them. Although she'd been surprised when she first met them, she'd become so used to tiny people who looked like chubby, bald-headed babies that she no longer thought they were unusual.

Cory was seated at her desk and had just begun to fill out the leaf work when Orville knocked on the open door. The head butler and one of Cory's favorite putti, he was in charge of making sure that the household ran smoothly. When Cory waved him in, he toddled to her desk carrying a tray and saying, "Lunch won't be for another two hours, so I brought you a sandwich."

Cory grinned as he set a plate and a glass of juice in front of her. Flying long distances didn't tire her out, but it always left her with a raging appetite. She was about to take her first bite when Orville handed her a leaf. "I also brought the menu for tonight if you'd care to read it," he said.

Cory reached for the leaf. She had enjoyed taking care of her uncle's house while she lived with him. Cooking and cleaning had been ways to thank him for letting her stay there. They also kept her busy when she wasn't making matches, or doing odd jobs for people or drumming with her band, Zephyr. Moving into the big house and becoming Cupid had changed a lot of things in Cory's life. Now the putti handled all the cleaning, and the excellent chef, Creampuff, did all the cooking. Cory no longer did odd jobs for anyone, and the only matches she made were because of her visions, not because people had hired her to do them. She was still playing with Zephyr, however. It was something she swore she'd never give up. When she had the time, she'd also started to write songs on her own.

Orville waited while Cory glanced at the menu. Although she had enjoyed cooking, she knew that the putti chef's food was a hundred times better. After reading the menu, she was already looking forward to supper.

"It looks perfect," she told Orville. She was smiling at him when a vision of two very ugly ogres with oddly shaped heads and large, hairy warts came to her. She knew that other ogres would consider them very attractive, but Cory thought they were almost frightening.

"Will you be leaving soon?" asked Orville. All the putti knew that when Cory got a certain look in her eyes, she was having another vision.

Cory nodded. "But not until I've eaten this," she said, and took a bite of her sandwich.

>>→

Cory was off making more matches until late afternoon. When she came back, she tried to hurry through the leaf work before her uncle, Micah, and his fiancée, Quince, arrived. She was looking forward to seeing Micah again and getting to know Quince.

Setting the leaves in the basket for Sarilee to collect, Cory hurried to her room to change her clothes. She loved the bedroom and adjoining bathing room that she'd chosen, as well as the fact that she didn't have to share either one with anyone other than Shimmer. After brushing her hair and changing into a new green dress made of silk, she hurried to the stairs.

Cory was partway down the elegant staircase when the door opened and Blue walked in. Johnny Blue was half ogre, half human. He was over seven feet tall, which was short for an ogre, and tall for a human. He also had a rough, craggy face, which many people found unattractive, but he was handsome in Cory's eyes. He was an officer-in-training at the Fey Law Enforcement Agency, or FLEA, as most people called it. More importantly, he was Cory's very own true love. Like Macks, he had a room on the first floor of the big house and was there when Cory needed him. Protecting the love of his life was his top priority.

Blue looked up and saw Cory. Opening his arms, he waited as she ran down the last few steps and into his embrace. They kissed, and Cory knew that whatever else might happen, everything was all right as long as he was there.

"Ahem!" Orville was standing by the door to the hallway. "Beverages are being served on the back terrace," he announced before walking away.

"I got called into the chief's office today," Blue said as he and Cory walked hand in hand toward the terrace. "It seems that I've put in enough hours and my work has been good enough that I don't have to wait the full year to take the Culprit Interrogator test."

"That's wonderful!" Cory cried. "Congratulations!"

"I'm afraid it means that I'll have to spend most of my free time studying. The test is next month."

"Then I'll tell everyone to be extra quiet around you so you can concentrate," Cory told him.

"Why do we need to be quiet around Blue?" her grandfather asked as he joined them in the hallway.

"He's going to be studying for his CI test!" Cory replied. "Isn't that wonderful!"

"It is indeed," said Lionel. "But I must say that I'm not surprised. I've heard only good things about your work, young man. Imagine, a CI in the family!"

Although Cory and Blue were waiting until they were older, everyone knew that they were going to get married someday. The only family member who hadn't given them her blessing was Cory's mother, Delphinium, who didn't seem to approve of anything Cory had done once she'd quit the Tooth Fairy Guild.

Cory, Blue, and Lionel had just accepted glasses of berry juice from the putti carrying a tray when Micah and Quince walked through the glass doors onto the terrace. Cory hadn't seen her uncle since the day she moved out of his house. Setting her glass on a table, she hurried to give him a welcoming hug. "It's so good to see you!" she told him.

"You too!" he replied. "How is everything?"

"Busy," Cory said, and turned to Quince. It felt natural to give her a hug, too.

"I've been looking forward to meeting you!" said Quince. "A few minutes in my office doesn't count," she added with a laugh. "How is your woodchuck doing, by the way?"

Quince, a chiropractor for animals, had treated Weegie, the woodchuck, for a sore back. Cory had *seen* Quince in a vision, and knew that she'd finally found the match for Micah.

"She's fine," Cory said. "Actually, we have two wood-chucks living with us. Weegie and Noodles have dug a den in the woods down by the river."

"Go long!" Macks shouted to Shimmer as they came around the house. The ogre threw a ball and the baby dragon shot after it, catching the ball with her front talons.

Quince gasped when she turned and saw them. "Micah said you had a baby dragon! She's adorable!"

"And very talented," said Lionel.

Micah was introducing his fiancée to Cory's grandfather when Orville toddled out of the house. "If you would all care to come inside, dinner will be served shortly," he announced.

"Good, because I'm famished," Cory said. Taking Blue's hand, she started for the door.

"Any idea what we're having tonight?" Blue asked her.

"Stir-fried vegetables," said Cory. "And roast beef for people who like meat."

Ogres loved meat and Blue was half ogre. He'd been doing without it lately because Cory had been raised as a fairy and was still a vegetarian. She appreciated Creampuff's efforts to make everyone happy.

"Roast beef, huh?" Blue said, and smacked his lips. "That chef sure knows the way to a man's heart!"

Cory laughed. "Should I be jealous?"

"Never," Blue said as he picked her up and spun her around. "I'd take you over roast beef any day!"

Because there were only five of them, they ate in the family dining room. Cory was enjoying her vegetables when Quince turned to her and said, "I have a favor to ask of you. Would you be my maid of honor? It would mean a lot to Micah and to me if you were part of our wedding."

"I'd be delighted!" Cory cried. "And if there's anything I can do to help, just let me know."

"I was hoping you'd say that," said Quince. "The wedding is only a week and a half away. I thought I could handle it all, but I'm getting a little overwhelmed."

"Actually, I might be able to help," said Lionel. "I was wondering if you two would like to hold your wedding here. You can have it inside if it rains or on the back lawn if it's sunny. Either way, you can invite as many people as you'd like. Creampuff would be happy to prepare all the food."

"That's a very kind offer," Micah told him, "but Quince and I have already decided that we want to have a simple wedding in the park across the street from my house."

"I'd be happy to help you with whatever you need," Cory told Quince. "Let me know what you want me to do and—"

A high, thin shriek made everyone look around. It seemed to be coming from the fireplace. When the sound faded, Lionel gestured to Orville and said, "Please go find out what made that awful racket."

"Of course, sir," said Orville. He was back a few minutes later. "It appears that Shimmer lit her fire under some fairies who were attempting to drop weasels down the chimneys."

"How odd," said Lionel. "I wonder why they chose weasels."

"I think I can answer that," said Blue. "When I finally caught up with the fairies who had brought rats to the Shady Nook when Zephyr was performing, one of them told me that they had paid a deposit on the rats, hoping to collect them and take them back to the rental shop the next day. The fairy was irate that the shape-shifter in the audience had turned into a cat and eaten them all. I can only assume that the shop was out of rats and the fairies who came by just now thought that weasels were the closest thing."

"Do you think they paid a deposit on the weasels, too?" asked Cory. "What kind of a shop rents such things anyway?"

"A vermin rental shop, I suppose," said Lionel.

"Are the fairies still coming after you?" Micah asked Cory. "I thought they would stop after the guilds lost the trial."

"I think losing just made them madder," said Cory. "Macks patrols the grounds with Shimmer off and on all day. Ever since the trial he's chased away a couple of dozen fairies who were trying to do something nasty. The poor putti who takes care of the garden is forever pulling up poison ivy and thistles that the flower fairies keep planting."

"The flower fairies have been especially mad ever since Flora Petalsby, the head of their guild, was sent to jail," said Blue.

"What about the Tooth Fairy Guild?" asked Micah. "Have you heard anything from Delphinium?"

Cory shook her head. "Mother doesn't want to talk to me any more than I want to talk to her now. If I'm lucky, it will stay that way for a very long time. I doubt that I'll be invited to her wedding, whatever kind she chooses."

CHAPTER
2

*Y*ou said a few days ago that I had money for whatever I need," Cory said to her grandfather. "Is it all
right if I buy Micah a new rug? I owe him one after
Noodles chewed a hole in the old one."

"Of course, my dear," said her grandfather. "Micah
and Quince can pick out whichever rug they want. Newlyweds shouldn't start their lives together with holes in
their rugs. And you don't have to confer with me about
your money. You have earned it and it is yours to spend
however you wish."

Blue had already gone to the FLEA station, so
Cory and her grandfather were the only ones eating
breakfast on the terrace. Unless a vision interrupted
them, it was the most peaceful time of day for them
both.

"Did you have any visions last night?" her grand-father asked.

Cory nodded. "Two. I'm going to go through the books after breakfast to see if I can find them."

With so many matches to make, most of the people Cory *saw* were people she'd never met before. Fortunately, her grandfather kept an extensive collection of yearbooks with pictures, as well as all the public and not-so-public listings of people and their occupations in all the major towns in the land of the fey. Cory was about to ask for suggestions on where to look first, when she noticed Weegie and Noodles galumphing across the lawn, heading her way.

"Somebody with real big shoes was in our woods last night," Weegie said as she hopped onto the terrace. "We didn't see them at the time, but we found the foot-prints this morning. Noodles and I'll keep our eyes open for whoever it was in case he comes back. Just thought you should know." The woodchuck was starting to turn away when Noodles grumbled at her. "Oh, yeah. Noo-dles wanted me to tell you that whoever it was smells really bad."

Cory sighed. "If it's not one thing, it's another. I wonder who it is this time?"

She watched the woodchucks meander back toward their den, stopping now and then to nibble tempting grass. A friend had given Noodles to Cory when the woodchuck was just a baby. Recently, Noodles had fallen for Weegie, a wild chuck who had lived in the park across the street from Micah's house. A witch needing directions had cast a spell on Weegie, which was why the woodchuck could talk. Cory was used to Noodles, who was a normal woodchuck. She was still amazed by how much a talking woodchuck had to say.

After Cory and her grandfather finished breakfast, she went to her office and started looking through the yearbooks. She was getting good at estimating ages from her visions, so most of her searches were getting easier. The first person she looked for was a young woman with distinctive blue hair. Cory found her in the third yearbook. Her name was Brook Waterford and she was only a few years older than Cory. Assuming from her name that Brook was a water nymph, Cory checked the employee list for the Public Water Department. She was not only on the list, but her picture was in the department newsletter for being employee of the month. Cory was in luck. When she looked at the rest of the pictures in the newsletter, she spotted the other person from her vision. Torrent Riversworth worked in a different division in the PWD. Getting them together so she could match them might not be too hard.

Cory wasn't nearly as fortunate with the people from her other vision. Although she found them in the year-books without too much difficulty, her luck ended there. Zarinda Scard and Darkin Flay had both been in the pre-witch program at the Junior Fey School. The problem was, Cory didn't have any lists for witches. Unless they worked for a public agency, she wasn't going to be able to find their names or what they were currently doing.

A chime sounded, announcing an arrival in the message basket. Cory picked it up right away.

> Cory,
>   If you aren't too busy, can you meet me at Dora's Dress Shoppe to look at gowns at 1:00 this afternoon?
>   Your future aunt,
>   Quince

Cory looked up the location of the dress shop. When she saw that it was only a few blocks from the PWD, she sent a message back.

> Quince,
>   I'll see you there!
>   Looking forward to being your niece,
>   Cory

When Cory opened her office door, she saw her assistant, Sarilee, walking down the hall. "Please tell Macks that I'm going out to make a match," she told the putti woman. "I'm meeting with Quince after that. I'm not sure what time I'll be back."

Sarilee whipped out her ink stick and made a note on a leaf. "Very good, miss," she said. "I'll let Macks know. And the forms for the match will be on your desk when you return."

Cory shook her head as she walked down the hall. Her life was getting more and more complicated. She'd never had to fill out forms before. As far as she knew, they didn't go anywhere other than Sarilee's files.

When Cory stepped out the front door, Macks was standing on the curved drive with his solar cycle, Lucille. He looked fierce in his troll skull–shaped helmet with its horns and drops of blood-red paint. The helmet he handed to Cory was one he had picked out for her. Pink with red and white hearts, it wasn't something Cory would have chosen, but she wore it so she wouldn't hurt his feelings.

Macks climbed onto his cycle first and waited for Cory to sit down behind him. Cory would have taken the pedal-bus if she could have, but it wouldn't have been safe with the guild members still trying to torment her.

"Where are we going?" asked Macks as they started down the drive.

"The Public Water Department building first," Cory told him. "I don't know how long I'll be there."

"That's all right," said Macks. "I brought my book so I can work on it while I wait."

Like most ogres, Macks liked mazes. He not only liked solving them, he liked creating them and was making a book of mazes for other ogres to solve. Cory had seen some of his mazes and thought they were really hard. Macks often said that he hoped they weren't too easy for his friends.

The solar cycle was silent as they drove through Lionel's neighborhood of big houses and large lawns, eventually turning onto a busier street that headed downtown. The PWD was in the center of town, so it took them a while to get there. Although a lot of people had recognized Cory before the trial, she had become even more famous since then, not only for the trial, but for being in the band Zephyr. Contrary to what some of the restaurant owners had thought, Zephyr had become even more popular after guild members harassed them during performances. When she and Macks drove by, more than one person raised their hands and waggled them as if they were beating drumsticks.

The Public Water Department was in one of the taller buildings downtown, so she spotted it when they were still blocks away. When Macks pulled up in front of it, she took off her helmet and handed it to him. "I'll be out as soon as I finish," she told him.

"No hurry," he told her, patting the book that was peeking out of his pocket.

When Cory stepped into the front lobby of the building, she stopped to look around. A large mural of a sylvan glade and a stream tumbling over rounded pebbles covered an entire wall. The floor was made up of blue tiles with a pattern that looked like crystal clear, sun-sparkled water. It made her feel as if she were standing on water and she was a little disoriented at first.

Trying not to look down, she walked across the floor, heading to the ladies' cleaning-up room. Being recognized for any reason would only make her job harder, so she hid her hair with a scarf and put on a pair of glasses she didn't need. She hoped that would be enough. When she left the room, she went straight to the directory on the wall. The division that Brook worked in was on the third floor; Torrent's division was on the second.

"How am I going to get them together?" she muttered to herself, earning a glance from a woman who was passing by.

Cory decided to look around and started walking to the back of the building. Along with the watery-looking tiles on the floor, there were framed pictures of water everywhere. She saw waterfalls, rivers, lakes, ocean waves, dew drops on leaves, falling rain, and even puddles. It wasn't long before she started to feel thirsty.

After passing a number of meeting rooms, she followed a group of people to the cafeteria. A large, bright room with lots of windows and a splashing fountain in the middle, it was a very appealing place to eat, especially for a group of water nymphs. A long line had already formed leading to the food tables, but it seemed to be moving quickly.

"Do most of the employees eat their lunch here?" Cory asked the woman at the end of the line.

"Just about everybody," she said. "The food is delicious and doesn't cost much. I eat here every day."

Cory nodded. This was the place to wait for Brook and Torrent, then. If it didn't work out, she'd have to find a way to bring them together some other day.

When Cory didn't see either of the nymphs from her vision, she got in line and bought a salad and a glass of juice. Taking a seat near the table where she'd paid, she watched the people coming out of the line. Although she saw a lot of nymphs with blue hair, as well as green, lavender, and all the colors a human might have, she didn't see anyone with Brook's shade of blue.

Cory was halfway through her salad when she saw Brook in the midst of a group of lady nymphs. Brook was talking and laughing with her friends when she passed Cory's table. Picking up her salad and drink, Cory moved to a table that was close to theirs, but where she could still see the end of the line.

Although Cory dawdled over her lunch, she finished without seeing any sign of Torrent. Fewer and fewer people were entering the cafeteria, and Cory was starting to think that she had wasted her time when Torrent finally walked in, deep in conversation with another male nymph. Cory glanced at Brook, who had just stood up and was collecting her trash. The nymph's friends were standing up as well, leaving Cory without a clear shot. She'd have to delay Brook until Torrent was a little closer.

Torrent was getting in line when Cory hurried to intercept Brook. Walking around some of the other nymphs, Cory pretended to bump into her. Acting surprised, she said, "Don't I know you? Brook Waterford, right?"

Brook looked at her and frowned. "I'm afraid I can't . . ."

"Don't tell me that you don't remember me!" Cory cried, even as she sneaked a glance at Torrent. He was coming down the line now, with only a few people blocking her view.

"You do look familiar . . . ," Brook said, frowning.

"Junior Fey School, remember?" said Cory.

"Uh," Brook said, her frown deepening.

Cory glanced at Torrent again. She sighed with relief when she saw that she finally had a clear shot.

Bow! she thought, holding out her hands. Time stood still as she reached for her first arrow.

It was after one o'clock when Cory walked out of the PWD. Macks was sitting on a bench outside the door, drawing a new maze.

"I'm late for my meeting with Quince," Cory said as they started toward Macks's solar cycle. "I was supposed to be at Dora's Dress Shoppe by one."

"I know where that is," said Macks. "Estel likes to look in the window when we go past. It isn't far from here."

"Maybe I should walk there," said Cory. "There aren't very many parking spots and you already have one for Lucille."

"It's all right," Macks said as he started the cycle. "There's a lot more spots by Dora's than there are here."

It took only a few minutes to drive to Dora's. Macks was able to get a parking spot in front of the store. "I'll stay right here with Lucille," he said, taking out his book. "Estel would never forgive me if she heard I went anywhere near Dora's without her."

Cory turned and looked at the store. Three bridal gowns were on display in the window; one was ogress-size, one was human- or nymph-size, and one would be just right for a sprite no taller than Cory's knees.

"So Estel likes to look at wedding dresses?" she asked Macks. "Is there something I don't know?"

Macks groaned and shook his head. "Not yet," he said. "I'm not ready to ask her and she knows it."

Cory was smiling when she walked into Dora's store. Her smile grew even broader when she saw Quince inside, looking at the human-size dresses.

"I'm sorry I'm late," Cory told her. "I had some business to attend to and it took longer than I'd expected."

"That's all right," Quince said. "There are so many dresses to choose from that I don't know how I'll ever make up my mind."

"Then it's good that I'm here," Cory told her. "It always helps to have a second opinion."

"That's not the only reason I wanted you to come today!" Quince said with a laugh. "We need to find you a dress, too!"

"Then let's start with yours," said Cory. "It is the most important dress, after all!"

The girls looked through the racks of human-size dresses together. They saw dresses with long sleeves and some with no sleeves. There were dresses with frills, lace, and sparkles, and some that were very plain. With Cory's help, Quince was able to pick out six dresses to try on. They were starting to look at bridesmaid dresses when a group of ogresses came out of the fitting rooms in the back. The bride was carrying a big, poufy bright-pink gown covered in ruffles, while her friends carried ruffled dresses in a bilious green.

"I'm so glad you found the perfect dress," said one of the bridesmaids. "You're going to look beautiful!"

"And the dresses you picked out for us are the most divine color!" said another ogress. "Who would have thought they'd have dresses the exact shade of your eyes."

Cory had to look away so they wouldn't see her grimace. She'd rather wear a fertilizer bag than a dress that shade of green.

Only a few minutes after the ogresses disappeared into the room where the seamstress worked, the door opened and a dozen lady sprites came in, bringing five of their children with them. While the knee-high adults crowded around the little racks of dresses at one side of the room, the tiny children began to play, running between the racks of bigger clothes and hiding between the floor-length dresses. Cory almost tripped over a little boy, and Quince let out a small shriek when a girl jumped out from between two dresses, giggling.

It took Cory a while to find one she liked. She pulled it off the rack and thought it was heavy. Turning the dress to look at the back, she found a sprite child swinging from the bow. Cory put the dress back. She wasn't much on bows anyway.

After finding three dresses to try, Cory decided she had enough. "Let's go try these on," she told Quince.

They went to the back of the big showroom to the even bigger area that was divided into individual fitting rooms. Cory went into one room, while Quince took the room next to it. Cory was trying on her second dress when two tiny girls peeped behind the curtain. "Mommy, there's a lady in here putting on a pink dress!" one of the girls cried out.

"That's nice, honey," said her mother.

"Please close the curtain," Cory told the children.

The little girls laughed and let the curtain drop. A moment later, when Cory heard Quince say, "You may not come in here!" the girls laughed again.

Cory settled on the peach-colored dress that she tried on next. After putting the other dresses on the rack outside the door, she went to the room that Quince was using. "I'm out here if you need any help," she told her.

"What do you think of this one?" Quince said, opening the curtain.

"I love it!" said Cory.

Quince grinned. "Great! I do, too. I don't look good in ruffles or flounces."

The pale blue dress was simple, yet elegant. Cory agreed that it was the best choice.

After picking out shoes to match their dresses, they visited the seamstress's station, where a dwarf was waiting to help. She was pinning Quince's gown so it would fit perfectly when Cory noticed that the sprite children had followed them into the room. "Shoo!" Cory said.

The children giggled and ran behind the curtain, but Cory could still hear them. Cory's dress didn't take long to pin, and paying for the dresses was even faster. The only problem came when the female elf behind the counter asked for the day they needed the gowns. When Quince told her, the girl said, "That doesn't give our seamstress much time, not with all the other gowns she has to alter. We'll have to deliver them to you the day of the wedding. Here, give me all your information and we'll make sure they get there on time."

Quince filled out the information cards. A minute later, Quince and Cory were standing in front of the store.

"I still need to pick out my flowers," said Quince. "I'm getting artificial ones for my bouquet. Would you like to go with me?"

Cory shook her head. "I'd better not, considering how much some members of the Flower Fairy Guild still hate me. You'll be better off if I don't go. Oh, and you don't need to worry about the cake. Creampuff will be very disappointed if you don't let her make it."

"We wouldn't want that!" Quince told her. "I'll be happy to have anything she'll make. Creampuff is a wonderful chef!"

"I should go now," said Cory. "I still have work to do and Zephyr is playing at the Shady Nook tonight. You and Micah should come hear us sometime. Let me know when you're available and I'll see that you get in. Jack Horner is selling tickets ahead of time now and they've all been selling out."

"We'd love to hear you play," Quince told her. "I'll talk to Micah about it."

The girls said good-bye, and Cory started toward Macks, who was still waiting by his solar cycle. They were heading home when the vision of the two witches she was supposed to match formed in Cory's mind. She'd have to find them somehow. There had to be some record of where they worked.

When Macks pulled up in front of the house, Laudine Kundry waved to Cory from the yard next door. Macks was parking Lucille when he said, "Why don't you go talk to your neighbor? I'm going to see if Creampuff can whip up something for my lunch. Do you want anything?"

"No thanks, I'm fine," Cory said, feeling guilty that she had eaten lunch and he hadn't. She started across the lawn and met Laudine partway.

"I need to talk to you," said Laudine. "I caught some frost fairies hiding in my trees while they spied on your house. I used a temporary 'turn-to-stone' spell on them in case you want to question them or turn them in to the FLEA."

"I think being turned to stone for a while is enough punishment," said Cory. "You can let them go. I doubt they'll be back now that they know that you're my neighbor."

"Good enough," said Laudine. "I also wanted to tell you that both Serelia and I have been trying to find out who was behind the incident with the kraken. Neither of us have had any luck so far."

Both Laudine, the head of Witches United, and Serelia Quirt, one of the strongest members of the Water Nymph Guild, had been eating lunch in Cory's backyard when a kraken attacked from the river. No one had been hurt because of the quick thinking of both women.

"We may never find out who did it," Cory told her. "I just wish the guild members would stop pestering me. Most of the guilds are leaving me alone now, but the fairies can really hold a grudge."

"They aren't the only ones," said Laudine. "Some witches are like that, too. I've been president of WU for over forty years. There's a faction in my guild that has been wanting to depose me for nearly that long because I told them they couldn't terrorize people for fun. I said that they have to have a legitimate reason and fill out application forms in triplicate. Most witches don't want to bother with the leaf work, so witch-related violence has dropped by over half since I took office. This faction would love to take over, but it would change all the rules and damage the guild's reputation. It would turn a lot of people against us. Hagatha Smerch is their leader. We used to be friends back when she was still Sarabeth, before she changed her name to Hagatha. She used to be such a nice girl, too."

They turned toward the street as someone rode past on a solar cycle. "You know, Hagatha and her friends have been asking me about you, Cory," Laudine continued. "They want to know why I'm sure you're not using unlicensed love magic, but I can't tell them. You really locked in that promise I made not to reveal that you're a Cupid. I can't even mention your name to anyone but the people in your household."

"I'm sorry it's made your life more difficult," Cory said.

Laudine shrugged. "I'm the head of the most powerful witches' guild. Things are always popping up to make my life difficult."

"Talking about guilds," said Cory. "Would you have a list of your guild members? I'm trying to match up two witches, but I have no idea how to find them."

Laudine's sour expression brightened. "Matching two witches! How wonderful! Unlike some witches, I believe in true love. I have ever since your grandfather matched me to the love of my life. I'm not supposed to hand out the membership list, but I'll make an exception for this. And if there's ever any other way I can help you make a match, just let me know!"

CHAPTER
3

C ory didn't have a chance to look at the WU membership list until late that afternoon. When she was able to sit down and study the names of the members of Witches United, she finally found Zarinda Scard and learned that she taught at a preschool for young witches. Although Cory looked through the list three times, she couldn't find Darkin Flay.

Cory was filing leaf work when Sarilee came to her door. "There's someone here to see you. I had him wait on the back terrace."

"Who is it?" Cory asked as she got to her feet.

"He says his name is Melter," said her assistant. "He's awfully big and furry. I think he smells like a wet dog. Orville said that your visitor has big feet."

"Orville probably meant that Melter is a Bigfoot," Cory said, and hurried out the door.

She found the Bigfoot sitting on the terrace steps looking out over the lawn and the river beyond. "You have a great view," he said when he saw Cory. "And two very polite woodchucks."

"I'm glad they were polite," Cory said with a laugh. "They aren't always."

Melter shrugged. "I met them when I had lunch at your house after I was sent to terrorize you. We had a nice conversation and got along pretty well. Forest animals usually like me. We have a lot in common," he said, scratching his furry side. "Anyway, I was back in town and thought I should tell you some of the rumors I've heard. The Itinerant Troublemakers Guild is no longer taking requests to send its members to your house. This new house is very nice, by the way." He turned to admire it and sighed. "I wish I could afford something like this."

"It's my grandfather's, actually," said Cory.

"Ah! That explains it," he said, nodding. "So I stopped by the house where you used to live. A witch who says she's a friend of yours tried to turn me into a tree until I told her that I'm your friend, too. She gave me your address and sold me a candle she'd just made. She said she'd bought some, but they didn't work as well as she wanted, so she decided to make her own. She has eleven different scents so far. I bought the one that smells like pine. She says they'll get rid of flies. Or was it fleas? Either one will be good."

"That was probably my friend Wanita. She's really into candles. Was there something else you wanted to tell me about the ITG?" said Cory.

"Oh, right. Word is out that someone keeps asking them to send more Big Baddies after you. Headquarters isn't doing it, of course, but there's still a problem. Some of the old contracts on you haven't been fulfilled yet, and the BBs haven't checked in, so they don't know the contracts are null and void."

"So they still might be coming after me," said Cory.

"Yup," Melter said. "Keep in mind that most Big Baddies who've heard about Franklin wouldn't go after you now, even if the contracts were still in effect. You know—Franklin the kraken? Some of the knots that witch tied are permanent."

"Really? I'll have to tell Laudine," said Cory. "I can't say I'm sorry, though. He was trying to kill us."

"Oh, I don't know if he'd have gone that far," said Melter. "We were just supposed to scare you. It was all a big show."

"Which seemed very real at the time," Cory told him. "I'm sorry, but I have to go change my clothes. I'd invite you to stay for dinner except I'm not eating until after the show. I'm in a band called Zephyr and we're performing tonight."

"That's okay. I'm staying with my cousin who lives just outside of town. He has a nice big den with a couch that has my name on it. I wrote it there yesterday. I wonder if he's noticed my signature yet. Anyway, he's expecting me for dinner, so I should get going."

"I'll walk you out front," said Cory.

They were starting around the side of the house when Shimmer came flying back from the river. The baby dragon had a fish flopping between her jaws. Seeing Cory, Shimmer opened her mouth to call to her, and dropped the fish. Before it could hit the ground, the dragon swooped down and scooped it up, only to swallow it whole.

"Watch out!" cried Melter. "Someone sent a dragon after you!"

Cory laughed. "That's my dragon, Shimmer. She's still just a baby."

The little dragon flew straight into Cory's arms, making happy sounds. Cory held her close with one arm and scratched Shimmer's head with her free hand.

"Was that fish your dinner or just a snack?" Cory asked her.

"A dragon, huh? I have a pet hedgehog at home," said the Bigfoot as they continued walking. "I really miss Spike!"

"I think Shimmer is more of a friend than a pet," said Cory.

When they reached the front yard, Melter stopped to say, "I just want you to know that I have no idea which Big Baddies might be coming after you, so you should be careful."

"I will," said Cory. "Thank you for the warning. It was nice of you to come tell me."

"Good luck!" Melter said, and headed to the street.

Cory had just turned around to go back inside when she heard someone calling to her, "Oh, Miss Feather-ing! Yoo-hoo! Over here!"

Cory turned toward the voice and saw an older fairy woman with blue hair waving to her from the other side of the lawn. She had never met the neighbors on that side and didn't know anything about them. Perhaps it was time to introduce herself, although they did seem to know her name.

Cory started across the lawn, still holding Shimmer. "Hello," she said when she reached the fairy woman.

"I've been so wanting to meet you!" the woman told her. "I'm Thrush Thistlethwaite and this is my husband, Thorny Thistlethwaite." She gestured to an older fairy who was watering the garden. He glanced at Cory and grunted, then moved farther down the lawn.

"I know you're Lionel's granddaughter, but I'm afraid I don't know your first name."

"I'm Cory," she said. "It's nice to meet you."

"We've been living next to your grandfather for the last ten years—ever since Thorny invented the automatic pollen spreader and made his fortune. I'm sure you've heard of it—all the flower fairies use it now."

"I'm not familiar with—"

"Oh, good! Here's my daughter Poppy. I'm sure you've heard of her! She started a new guild with a friend of hers. It's very well known already—the Belly Button Lint Guild. You and my Poppy are probably around the same age. Just think—you can be friends, too! Poppy dear, her name is Cory, just like you thought, but she hasn't told me any more than that. I'll leave you girls to talk. There are things I need to do inside."

"So you're Cory Feathering!" said Poppy. "I've heard a lot about you. Very little of it was good. You sure did a number on the guilds."

"It wasn't anything they didn't deserve," said Cory. She already didn't like the girl, not only because of the snooty look on her face, but also because the Belly Button Lint Guild had sided with the Tooth Fairy Guild against Cory.

Shimmer started to make a deep-throated growl that shook her whole body. Apparently, the little dragon didn't like Poppy, either.

"I don't like the way that dragon is looking at me," said Poppy. "Does it bite?"

"I've never seen her bite anything but her food," Cory replied. "She doesn't need to. She has a very hot flame."

Shimmer shifted in her arms as if she was getting ready to demonstrate. Poppy took a step back. "I don't think people should be allowed to own dragons," said Poppy. "They're very dangerous."

"Shimmer is dangerous only to people who mean me harm, or who come to my house to cause trouble. You don't know anyone like that, do you?"

"No, of course not!" Poppy declared, backing away again. "Tell me something. I've heard rumors that you're a matchmaker. Is it true?"

"I have helped some of my friends make matches in the past," Cory told her.

"If I paid you, would you make a match for me?" asked Poppy.

Cory shook her head. "I'm not doing that anymore." *At least not the way I used to,* Cory added silently. "You'll have to excuse me," she told Poppy. "I need to go. I'm sure I'll see you soon."

"I'm sure you will," said Poppy.

As Cory walked away, Shimmer wiggled around until she was looking behind them. When the dragon hissed, Cory patted her back, saying, "I don't trust that girl, either. We'll have to keep our eyes on her."

Cory rode on the back of Blue's solar cycle to the Shady Nook, while Macks and his girlfriend, Estel, rode Lucille. A group of ogres riding solar cycles joined them on the road when they were almost there. Cory liked ogres, but they drew so much attention that she felt as if they were in a parade when everyone on the streets stopped to stare. She couldn't help but notice that while many people they passed smiled and waved, some of the fairies gave her dirty looks.

After the ogres parked their cycles, they went in to find seats. "Go on ahead," Macks told Estel. "Get a good seat and save one for me. I need to do a security check before Cory goes in."

Estel pointed to the guards at the door. "The restaurant owner is already taking care of security, so I don't know why you have to do it, too. I didn't come here to sit by myself."

"I won't be long," Macks told her. "You know it's part of my job."

"And I'm your girlfriend!" Estel cried, stomping her foot. "I should come before your job! If you were a real ogre, you'd put me first. My grandfather never had a job and my grandmother always came first. He'd go on rampages and come back with whatever she wanted."

"That was a long time ago, sweetie!" Macks said. "People don't do that anymore."

"Don't 'sweetie' me!" said Estel. "I'm going inside."

"Are you and Estel okay?" Cory asked as the ogress stomped off.

Macks shrugged. "A friend of hers saw me outside Dora's Dress Shoppe when I was waiting for you. She asked Estel if she had been looking at wedding gowns. Estel blew up when she heard that I was there because of my job. Now I can't seem to do anything right. Excuse me, I'd better go in and do my security sweep so I can go sit with Estel."

"I seem to be making everyone's life harder these days," Cory said to Blue. "First Laudine, now Macks."

"Macks and Estel will be fine," Blue told her as they walked toward the entrance. "They fight like that all the time."

Cory wasn't so sure when Macks came out to get her a few minutes later. "You can go in now," he said, but his face looked grim, and he followed Blue to a seat near the stage. Cory looked for Estel and saw her seated with the other ogres. Apparently, she hadn't saved Macks a seat after all.

The band played well that night. They started with "Morning Mist," then played "Storm-Chased Maid" and "Shooting Stars." The ogres got rowdy during "Thunder's Clap," but no one seemed to mind. After a break, Zephyr played "Owl Goes A-Hunting" and other older songs, then finished the night with everyone's favorite, "Summer Heat." Cory noticed that when audience members acted as if they really were feeling the heat of summer, the waiters served a lot more drinks.

When the band finished playing and the audience was leaving, Jack Horner, the owner of the restaurant, came to the platform to talk to Olot, the ogre and bandleader. "That was great!" Jack said. "I would have a packed house every night if Zephyr was playing. I'd like to show my appreciation tonight and offer you folks dinner. Are you interested?"

Olot turned to the band members. When they all nodded, he grinned and said, "Sure! Playing like that always makes me hungry."

"Excellent!" said Jack. "Then you finish packing up and I'll have my people get your table ready."

Macks came up to Cory while she was covering her drums. "If you're going to stay, do you mind if I take Estel home?"

"Go ahead," Cory told him. "Blue and I will be fine."

"Thanks!" Macks said, and hurried off to find Estel.

The waiters put together enough tables that the whole band and their friends could sit together. Cory and Blue sat at the end near Olot, his wife, Chancy, and Jack Horner. The waiters brought out one dish after another. Olot had just filled his plate when Jack Horner turned to him and said, "I've been thinking about sponsoring a Battle of the Bands. Do you think your band would be interested?"

Olot looked puzzled. "Why would we want to fight other bands?"

Jack laughed, but he stopped when he saw that Olot looked serious. "I can see why an ogre would think that! Actually, it's a competition. You play your music and the other bands play theirs. The audience decides which band is the best. A fairy friend of mine heard about it in the human world. I thought it sounded like a good way to show everyone just how great Zephyr is."

"When are you planning this 'Battle'?"

"As soon as I can make the arrangements," said Jack. "We'll hold it in one of the big parks."

"Then we'll be there. Anything to get Zephyr's name out," Olot told him.

"Good enough!" Jack replied. "I'll see if there's a park available."

Cory and Blue left the restaurant at the same time as Chancy and Olot, although a number of band members stayed behind. Blue had just turned his cycle onto Lionel's street when Cory said, "What do you think of that Battle thing? I think it sounds like fun."

"I think it sounds like a real security problem," said Blue. "It's one thing to perform indoors, where we can control who's coming and going. Even ogre parties held outside aren't hard because we can spot anyone who isn't an ogre. But a big event in a park with all sorts of bands and all sorts of people there . . . I don't know how we'd handle security for that."

"Lots of ogre guards?" said Cory.

"Maybe," said Blue.

He parked his solar cycle in front of the house. They were just getting off when they heard a sound in the woods between their lawn and Laudine's. When she turned to look, Cory saw a big, dark figure half hidden in the gloom under the trees. "Macks, is that you?" she called.

At the sound of her voice, the figure lumbered away. "That isn't Macks," Blue said under his breath. "Stay here. I'll be right back."

Cory waited nervously in the glow of the fairy light coming from the front porch. Only a few minutes later, Blue was back, shaking his head. "Whoever it was took off before I could catch him."

"Did you get a good look at him?" asked Cory.

"Just enough to see that something isn't right. His movements are really jerky and the shape of his head is all wrong."

"I wonder if that was one of the Big Baddies that Melter warned me about," said Cory. "It might even be the person that the woodchucks told me about this morning."

"Melter was here? It seems as if you've had a number of conversations that you didn't tell me about," said Blue.

"You're right, I have," Cory said, taking his hand as they started toward the house. "How about a nice cup of hot chocolate and I'll tell you all about my day?"

CHAPTER

4

*B*lue didn't have to go into the FLEA station the next morning, and Cory was looking forward to spending a leisurely day with him. She went downstairs expecting to see him seated with her grandfather on the terrace, but instead she found Orville waiting for her. "You'll be eating breakfast in the small dining room today," he told her, and started down the hall. "Lionel and Blue are already there."

"Why aren't we eating on the terrace?" she asked as she walked into the room. "It's a beautiful day."

"I wanted to eat in here," said her grandfather. "Change is nice now and then."

Both Blue and her grandfather looked at her as if they expected her to protest, but she just shrugged and took her seat. Even when they served themselves from the platters Orville brought to the table, they kept casting sideways glances at Cory. She thought they were both acting oddly, although she couldn't figure out why.

Cory was eating a muffin when there was a loud bang and a muffled shout outside the window. She started to get up to go look, but Blue said, "It's nothing. Have I told you about the case involving three vagrant mermaids?"

Cory was distracted until she heard a *thud*. "What was that? You can't say it was nothing!"

"Just Macks playing with Shimmer," her grandfather said, reaching out to pat her hand. "Here, have you tried the fried pickles?"

They had almost finished eating when Cory turned to Blue and said, "This is your first day off since we moved in with Grandfather. Why don't we go for a walk along the river after breakfast?"

"Actually," said Lionel, "I was going to ask you to show me the notes about the matches you've been making, Cory. Sarilee tells me that you've had some interesting cases."

"I have, but it's such a beautiful day and—" Cory began.

"I can't go anyway," Blue hurried to say. "Macks and I are planning to discuss security for the Battle of the Bands."

"Oh," Cory said, disappointed. "In that case I'd be happy to go over my cases with you, Grandfather. Perhaps you can tell me how you would have handled some of the trickier situations I've encountered."

"I'd be delighted!" Lionel said. When they heard voices outside, he set down his napkin and stood. "We should get started. Blue, why don't you go see if Macks needs help?"

"Playing catch with Shimmer?" asked Cory. "Or going over security?"

"Whatever he needs," said her grandfather, and ushered her out of the room.

Cory's new office was down the hallway and around the corner. Even from the other end of the hallway, she could hear a disturbance in the kitchen. "I wonder what that's all about," she remarked.

"Creampuff must be in a bad mood," said Lionel, hustling her into her office and shutting the door behind them.

"You and Blue are acting awfully strangely," Cory said as she took her seat behind the desk.

"Not at all!" her grandfather declared. "Now, where are those notes?"

Cory didn't mind digging out all the information she had on her matches, but she thought it was odd that Lionel asked to hear every little detail. When she finished telling him everything she could think of, he started to regale her with stories of the more interesting matches he had made. He told her about matching two mermaids, and the time he had to match a harpy and an ogre.

"There were a few times I wasn't able to make the match. Once, I *saw* a vision of two trolls," Lionel told her. "I don't know anything about trolls or how to locate a particular pair, so I—"

There was a knock on the door and Orville peeked into the room. When he nodded, Lionel stood abruptly and turned to Cory. "Why don't we go for a walk now, my dear?" he asked, offering her his arm.

Cory frowned. There was something up, but she couldn't imagine what it might be. Taking his arm, she let him guide her down the hallway and out onto the terrace facing the river. It was almost as if she had stepped into a painting. Tables and chairs dotted the lawn and in between them stood most of her friends, silently waiting for her. And then they all shouted, "Happy birthday!" and the illusion was broken.

"You're throwing a party for me?" Cory said, turning to her grandfather. "I forgot it was my birthday. My mother never paid much attention to them. I've never had a birthday party before."

"You live here now and I consider birthdays to be a real reason to celebrate!" Lionel explained. "Why don't you go down there and greet some of your friends? You'll be surprised by how many people want to wish you well."

As Cory descended the steps and started across the lawn, the first person to approach her was her friend the witch Wanita, who was one of Micah's neighbors. Wanita had brought her pet boar, Theo, with her.

"Happy birthday!" Wanita cried, throwing her arms around Cory. "I haven't seen you in ages!"

"It hasn't been that long," said Cory as Wanita continued to hug her.

"Well, it seems like it," Wanita said, letting her go. "Theo and I have missed you."

The boar grunted and started to gnaw on one of Wanita's already-chewed boots.

"The old neighborhood hasn't been the same without you," said Wanita. "It's much quieter now. No ogre motorcycle gangs showing up, or members of the Itinerant Troublemakers Guild lurking around, or fairies planting graffiti in yards."

"It sounds nice and quiet," Cory told her.

Wanita snorted. "Too quiet if you ask me. I liked it a lot better when you were there. Say, I've been hearing rumors that some of the guild members are still mad and haven't stopped coming after you. Is it true?"

"Yes, unfortunately," said Cory. "But it isn't anything we can't handle."

Wanita leaned over to peer behind Cory. "Is that the three little pigs? I didn't know they were coming. And it looks as if Alphonse has brought his girlfriend, what's her name. Theo's been getting a weird rash. I want to ask the brothers if it's common among pigs."

As Wanita scurried off, dragging Theo behind her, Salazar the genie walked up. Although he hadn't brought his pet iguana, he wasn't alone. He had a girl with him who looked as if she was only a few years younger than Cory. With her slightly tilted, deep purple eyes and long, silky black hair, she was exotic and very beautiful.

"Happy birthday, Cory," Salazar said, handing her a bouquet of roses.

"Thank you, Salazar," said Cory. "These are lovely!"

"I thought I owed you flowers, considering how many of yours my iguana, Boris, ate. I'd like to introduce you to my niece, Zara. She's about to start genie training."

"I've heard so much about you!" Zara told Cory. "I think you were very brave to stand up to the guilds the way you did!"

"I just did what I needed to do," Cory said with a shrug.

"Uncle Salazar says I might want to rethink going into genie training, but it's what I've always wanted. Both of my parents were genies and they loved it."

"Then it really is your family business," Blue said as he walked up and slipped his arm around Cory's waist. "It's great if it's a job you really want."

"I never really wanted to be a tooth fairy," Cory told her. "It just wasn't the job for me."

"Cory!" called Felice. She and her twin, Selene, were shape-shifters who could turn into leopards. They loved to confuse people by changing. Fortunately, Cory was used to them.

"We'll talk again later," Salazar said, and led his niece away as the two girls approached Cory and Blue.

"This is a great party! The food is fantastic!" said Selene.

Felice nodded. "We really loved the grilled trout, but we're saving space in case you'll let us go fishing off your riverbank."

"Would you mind?" asked Selene. "We haven't gone fishing in ages and we adore catching our own."

"I don't mind as long as you don't scare any of the guests," said Cory.

"We wouldn't dream of scaring anyone!" Selene said with a toothy grin.

Cory watched the girls run off toward the riverbank, passing the two long tables covered with platters and tureens. One table had been set up for vegetarians, the other for people who liked meat. A large group of ogres were already filling their plates from the meat-eaters table. Cory spotted Melter, the Bigfoot, talking to Macks, who didn't look very happy.

"I saw Olot and Chancy on the other side of the lawn," Blue told Cory. "All the band members are here."

"Good!" said Cory. "I'm glad they could come."

They started walking arm in arm, but they hadn't gone far before they ran into Laudine. "Did the list help?" she asked Cory.

"It did," Cory told her. "At least for one of the names. The other name wasn't on it."

"Who was it? Maybe I've heard of the person," said Laudine.

"Darkin Flay," said Cory. "Does the name sound familiar?"

Laudine shook her head. "No, but I can ask around."

"Thank you," said Cory. "That would help a lot. And thank you for sharing the list with me. I know you didn't have to."

"Are you joking? Everyone should help out when it comes to true love!" Laudine told her. "I'll come see you if I learn anything about this 'Darkin Flay.'"

As Laudine walked away, Blue bent down to whisper to Cory. "Is Laudine Kundry, the head of WU, helping you find your matches?"

Cory nodded. "She is if they're witches. Laudine is a true romantic at heart."

As Cory and Blue drifted through the crowd, they greeted Micah and Quince. "I have everything arranged for the wedding," Quince told Cory. "At least I hope I do. What if I've forgotten something?"

"Then we'll take care of it together," said Micah. "Don't worry, our wedding is going to be perfect!"

"Cory!" Olot boomed. "Happy birthday!"

Cory turned and found most of Zephyr grinning at her. "Happy birthday!" echoed Perky and Cheeble. Skippy and his two girlfriends waved.

"Did you hear that we're in the Battle of the Bands the day after tomorrow?" Cheeble asked her. The brownie's cheeks were pink with excitement, and his grin was so big that she could see all of his teeth. "I've already made three bets on us winning and I just learned this morning. I'll make even more bets today."

"I hadn't heard," said Cory.

"That's because I haven't had a chance to tell you yet," said Olot. "We're going to get together to rehearse first thing tomorrow morning and we'll be at it all day.

Don't worry about bringing a lunch. Chancy and I have it all planned."

"Free food tomorrow, too!" cried Cheeble. "This gets better and better!"

His glee was so obvious that Cory had to smile. "I'll be there," she said, but her smile faded when she saw the look on Perky's face. "Is everything all right?" she asked him.

"Everything is fine," he told her. "It's just that I got a message from Santa Claus right before I came here. He's headed back to the North Pole soon and wants me to go, too."

"Is that a problem?" said Cory.

"Not at all!' Perky replied. "I expected to go with him and would have been disappointed if he hadn't asked me. But I've gotten used to living here and I really enjoy playing with the band. I'm going to miss it a lot."

"Are you quitting the band now?" Cory asked.

"Not until right before we leave," Perky said. "I'm not sure when that'll be yet."

"You'll come back and visit us again though, won't you?" asked Cory.

"Sure! I'll be back next off-season," said Perky. "We're going to stay at the new beach house and I'll make a couple of trips to New Town to see all of you. And if you're ever visiting the North Pole you'll have to look me up!"

"The North Pole?" Blue said with a laugh. "I'll put it on my list!"

CHAPTER
5

Marjorie and Jack are headed this way," said Blue. "They have Stella with them."

Cory turned around. "Oh, good! We haven't seen any of them since we had dinner at Jack's house."

"How are you?" Stella cried as she took Cory's hand in hers. They had met when Cory was doing odd jobs for people, and had helped Stella can beans. After spending most of a day together they had become friends. One of Cory's first matches had been between Stella's son, Jack B. Nimble, and another friend, Marjorie Muffet.

"I'm well, thank you," Cory replied.

"I was so worried when I heard that the fairies were still pestering you," said Stella. "I've moved in with Jack, and his security is excellent. Even fairies don't trespass there."

"I installed a no-fly zone over my house," said Jack. "Actually," he added in a quieter voice, "I've hired goblins armed with peashooters to go after anyone who tries to fly over my walls. It's a lot more effective than you might think."

"We have ogre security," Blue replied. "It's very effective, too."

"I can imagine it would be!" said Marjorie.

"Did you see that Prince Rupert is here with his new bride?" Stella asked Cory. "I didn't know you knew them."

"Zephyr was playing at the castle the weekend they met," Cory told her. "I know the princess fairly well."

"Really?" Stella said, looking impressed.

"I didn't know that Rupert and Goldilocks were here," Cory said to Blue. "We should go greet them."

"They're in the middle of that group of people," Stella said, pointing.

"If you'll excuse us . . . ?" Cory said to her friends.

They all nodded and waved good-bye as Cory and Blue turned away. On their way to speak to the royal couple, Cory greeted Mary Lambkin and her new husband, Jasper, and waved to Gladys and six of her children. Reaching the edge of the group surrounding Rupert and Goldilocks, they found that they could do little more than catch a glimpse of the couple through the crowd of well-wishers and gawkers. Cory waved to Goldilocks, who waved back before turning away.

"Are you hungry?" Blue asked, steering Cory toward the tables of food.

"I am," Cory began. "I just don't—"

"There you are!" cried Cory's grandmother, Deidre. "Your grandfather and I have been looking all over for you. This is quite a crowd! And all the ogres! Did you see how hairy that one is? I thought it was an invasion when we first walked in. You do know how rowdy they can be? It never would have occurred to me to invite ogres to my house."

"Actually, they visit all the time," Cory told her grandmother. "Most of those ogres are friends of mine."

Deidre shook her head. "In my day, a young lady would never consort with people like that," she said, glancing from the ogres to Blue.

"Now Deidre," said Cory's grandfather.

"Is your mother coming?" Cory's grandmother interrupted. "I don't see her yet."

Cory turned to Blue. "No, she's not," he said. "She wasn't invited."

"Good!" declared Deidre. "My daughter is a real party pooper. And can you believe she's marrying a goblin? When she told me, I thought she was just being outrageous to make me mad, but she really is serious about it.

I always thought your mother was crazy, but now she's certifiable. Who in their right mind marries a goblin?"

"Another goblin?" said Cory.

Blue nudged Cory toward the line of people at the food tables. "Excuse us, please," he said. "We were just about to get something to eat."

"Oh, you should!" said Cory's grandfather. "Everything is delicious! I especially liked the asparagus salad."

"But I was still talking to them!" Deidre complained.

"You can talk to them later," said her husband. "Let the birthday girl get something to eat!"

Mouthing the words "thank you" to her grandfather, Cory let Blue hustle her to the vegetarian table before anyone else could stop them. "Go get in the other line," Cory told him. "I know how much you like meat. I'll see you after you get your food."

While Cory slowly advanced through the line, Blue headed to the other serving table. A few minutes later, Cory saw that Blue was talking to Macks, but there was no sign of Estel. When Cory looked around, she finally spotted the ogress deep in conversation with another ogre. After serving herself, Cory joined Blue on the hunt for seats at one of the many tables.

"Let's look over there," Blue said, indicating some tables closer to the river.

"I saw Estel talking to an ogre I've never met," Cory told him as they started to walk. "Do you know who he is?"

"That's Grog," said Blue. "He just moved here from the Deep Woods. Be careful around him. The ogres who live there are still mostly wild."

"Why isn't Estel with Macks?"

Blue leaned over to whisper in her ear. "They've had a big fight. Estel isn't speaking to Macks right now."

"Isn't this the kind of thing that can make an ogre go on a rampage?" asked Cory.

"It used to be, and sometimes still is," said Blue. "Macks is handling it really well."

They were only a few yards from the river when they found two seats at a table. To Cory's delight, Serelia Quirt was there, along with her water-nymph protégé Rina, Rina's parents, and her new baby brother.

"Hello!" Serelia said when she saw Cory and Blue. "Please, sit with us."

"Happy birthday!" said Minerva, Rina's mother. "This is a lovely party. The food is marvelous and the weather is perfect. To top it off, we even found a table by the water."

"It can't get any better than this," Rina's father agreed.

"I'm glad you could come," said Cory.

The baby squealed and flailed his pudgy arms.

"I haven't seen your new baby yet," Cory told them when Minerva started to rock him. "He's adorable!"

The baby found his fist. He sucked on it for a moment, then pulled it out and began to wail. "Pardon me," Minerva said over the crying baby. "I'm going to walk around a bit."

When she got up, her husband did, too, running after her with the diaper bag.

"How are your lessons going?" Cory asked Rina.

"Great!" the girl replied. "Serelia has taught me a lot!"

"She's a very quick learner," said Serelia, gazing fondly at Rina. "And a pleasure to teach."

"Whatever happened with your investigation into the kraken attack?" Blue asked.

Serelia sighed. "I still don't have a clue as to who was behind it. I hoped that the Water Nymph Guild would help, but they're dragging their feet."

"Serelia is going to run for president of the guild again," said Rina. "She was president a long time ago, but she thinks they need her even more now. The man who's running the guild is as useful as a leaky bucket."

Serelia laughed and patted the girl's hand. "We know where your loyalties lie! But it is true. I'm going to run for president and I—"

There was a loud splash and people seated beside the river started to talk in excited voices. "Did you see that? A leopard just caught a fish."

"There's another leopard over there!"

"I want to go see!" cried Rina.

As more people hurried to the water's edge, Serelia got to her feet. "Then let's go investigate," she said, taking the girl's hand.

Cory had just taken her first bite of food when Daisy arrived with a young man wearing a bowl-shaped haircut and a silver lip ring. Daisy had been Cory's friend since they were little girls. They were both members of Zephyr.

"Happy birthday, Cory!" Daisy exclaimed. "Imagine, your very first birthday party. I wanted to give you one when we were in Junior Fey School, but your mother wouldn't let me. She said there's no reason to celebrate getting older. We all have to do it, but we shouldn't pretend to be happy about it."

Taking a seat across from Cory, she pointed at the young man and said, "This is my new boyfriend."

The young man reached out to shake Blue's hand. "I'm Ptolomy Ptuttle," he said, pronouncing the Ps in his name.

"Ptolomy is a chef," said Daisy.

"I specialize in soups," he said. "I'm planning to open my own restaurant as soon as I can get the funds. I'm going to name it 'Soups On.' I don't suppose you'd like to be one of my backers? I have a great idea for Summer Soup. I'm going to include freshly mown grass and dandelions. They're the most summery things I know."

"What about strawberries?" suggested Cory.

"Great idea!" said Ptolomy. "Grass, dandelions, and strawberries! If I include strawberries, will you give me money? My restaurant is going to be a hit. My friends have been telling me so for years. I'm going to give Jack Horner and his Shady Nook their first real competition."

Cory had opened her mouth to reply, when Blue said, "Uh-oh. We're in for it now!"

When Cory turned around, she saw Grog kissing Estel. Macks was standing among a group of other ogres, his face turning redder and redder when he saw what Grog was doing.

Suddenly, all of Macks's self-control was gone. He went berserk, roaring at the top of his lungs, "Get your filthy paws off my girl!" A moment later he was on top of Grog, pounding him with both fists, while Estel stood to the side, watching open-mouthed. And then

Grog started to fight back, pummeling Macks as they rolled around on the ground.

While most of the crowd tried to get out of the way, the other ogres ran toward Macks and Grog. Two ogres tried to separate them, but went flying back when Macks punched them.

"I didn't know that Macks was that strong," Cory said to Blue.

"Ogres are exceptionally strong when they go on a rampage," Blue told her.

Melter and another ogre tried to pull Macks off Grog. Macks threw them both off his back. Melter crashed onto the table, and Blue and Ptolomy Ptuttle fell out of their chairs. When Ptolomy got up, he ran off, leaving Daisy to follow him.

Cory shook her head. Daisy never had been able to pick very good boyfriends or want to stay with them for long. Cory wondered what had happened with Jonas McDonald. She had introduced him to Daisy herself. Even though she knew they weren't a perfect match, he was far better than anyone Daisy ever chose. So far, Cory had been unable to *see* Daisy in a vision with any-one. When she tried again, she still couldn't *see* her friend's match. Even so, she wasn't going to give up.

"You sure throw a great party!" the Bigfoot told Cory as he stood and shook himself.

Cory looked back at Macks, who had pulled up a twenty-foot tree and was using it to club Grog. Rina screamed when Grog landed at her feet.

"That's enough of that!" Serelia said. Pointing at the river, she brought up a column of water, arcing it over the heads of the people in the crowd and dumping it full force on Macks. The ogre howled and sputtered as the water smashed him to the ground.

When the water finally let up and Macks got to his feet, dripping with water and blood, Estel ran to him, crying, "You really do love me!" and threw her arms around him.

A cheer went up from the crowd, and people began to applaud. Hearing this, Grog growled and looked as if he wanted to continue the fight, but five ogres and Melter picked him up and tossed him into the river.

Cory was helping Blue pick up pieces of the smashed table when she felt a tap on her shoulder. "I told you ogres were rowdy," said her grandmother. "Maybe next time you'll think twice about inviting them."

Deidre was walking away with a smug look on her face when Cory had a vision. This time she saw Macks and Estel, and knew that for once she might not need to do anything.

"Macks and Estel really are meant for each other," she told Blue.

Blue glanced at the two ogres, who were still kissing despite Macks's injuries. "I know. And I think they've finally figured it out, too."

"Yes, but I mean they're *really* meant for each other," said Cory.

"Did you *see* them in a vision?" Blue asked.

Cory nodded. "Just now. But I think this time I can leave it up to them. It looks as if they're doing fine on their own."

A familiar song began to play. Cory glanced at the house and saw that Zephyr had set up their instruments on the terrace. They had started with "Fairy Spring," a song that didn't require drums, but Cory knew that they would need her soon.

Alecks, Twark, and Skweely walked up and stopped in front of Cory. "We'll take care of the broken furniture," said Alecks, Macks's brother. "This is your birthday. You have better things to do."

The three ogres shooed Cory and Blue away, but they hadn't gone far when Cory spotted someone she didn't want to see. "Oh, no," she told Blue. "My mother just showed up."

"I was afraid she'd come even if we didn't send her an invitation," said Blue. "I know it's virtually impossible, but try not to let her upset you."

"I suppose there isn't time to hide in the crowd," Cory said, looking around.

"It's too late," Blue replied. "She's already headed this way. She brought Officer Deeds with her, too."

"I can't believe you had a party like this and didn't invite your own mother," Delphinium said in a voice meant to carry.

"Cory didn't send out the invitations," said Blue. "It was a surprise birthday party."

"I've been telling Delphinium that the invitation must have arrived in her message basket, but she threw it out by accident. That is what happened, isn't it?" said Officer Deeds, the goblin FLEA officer whom Cory had recently matched with her mother. Although he was shorter than Cory, the goblin's bulging forehead, long, crooked nose and bristling eyebrows made him appear formidable. The stern look he gave Blue was as strong as a command.

"Yes, of course, sir," said Blue.

"Humph!" said Delphinium. "I had to come see you sooner or later, Cory. Wilburton and I are going to have a traditional goblin wedding, so you'll have to be involved."

"I really don't think—" Cory began.

"I don't care what you think!" Delphinium declared. "All my female relatives have to take part. Now, I assume my mother is here. I have to tell her, too, and I might as well do it now."

"She never listens to me, does she?" Cory said to Blue as her mother walked away.

"Not since I've known her," Blue replied, shaking his head.

CHAPTER
6

*C*ory had to skip breakfast in order to get to band practice on time the next morning, and was still yawning when she climbed onto Macks's solar cycle, Lucille. "Creampuff sent this for you," Macks said, handing Cory a bag.

Cory peeked into the bag and took out a blueberry muffin. "Wonderful!" she said. "I'll have to thank her. Would you like some?"

When she offered the ogre the bag, he grinned and took one. "I got up extra early to eat breakfast, but I can always eat more of Creampuff's cooking. That putti sure can bake!"

It wasn't easy riding on the motorcycle and eating, but Cory managed. As they rode through the still-dark town, then up the mountain to Olot's cave, she started thinking about the song she'd been working on. She wondered if she should share it with her bandmates during rehearsal or wait for another day.

They had almost reached Olot's cave when she thought to ask Macks, "Are you going home again after you drop me off?"

"Not today," said Macks. "After you told me about the rehearsal, I offered to take Estel on a picnic. Don't tell anyone, but I'm going to propose. I figured we'd waited long enough."

"That's wonderful!" Cory told him. "Did you get her a ring?"

"Ogres don't wear rings," said Macks. "We get tattoos when we get married. It's part of the wedding ceremony. So is getting drunk and smashing things. I'd invite you, but I don't think you'd like it."

"I appreciate that," said Cory. "And you're right. That's one special occasion that I'd prefer to skip."

The sun was just coming up when Cory got off the solar cycle and got a good look at Macks's face. Grog had broken Macks's nose in the fight. It was swollen and he had two black eyes. He was also missing a front tooth. "Oh, Macks!" exclaimed Cory. "Does it hurt?"

"Naw, I hardly feel it," he said, but he winced when he touched his nose. "Estel says it makes me more handsome. She says she doesn't want me to get it fixed. It will always remind her how much I love her if I don't get it straightened."

"I'm glad you're marrying her," said Cory. "You two belong together."

"Are you saying that as a friend or as Cupid?" Macks asked.

"Both," Cory told him.

Macks grinned. "Then I know I'm doing the right thing! How long have you known?"

"Since yesterday," said Cory. "I had a vision of you and Estel during the party."

"I've been such a lunkhead," Macks said. "I should have proposed long before this!"

The door to the cave opened and Chancy looked out. "Oh, good! You're here. You're the last one to arrive."

"I have to go," Cory told Macks. "I don't know what time we'll be finished."

"No hurry," said Macks. "I'll be back by late afternoon. If you're not ready, I'll take a nap out here under the trees."

Everyone was tuning up when Cory followed Chancy into the cave. Olot's wife was already developing a baby bump and couldn't have looked happier. She pointed to a table where she'd set out doughnuts and pieces of fruit, but Cory wasn't hungry. Hurrying to her drum set, Cory started her warm-up exercises.

The band started with an old song, "Shooting Stars," then moved on to "The Last Flight of Silver Streak." They were partway through the song when a gong sounded and Chancy got up to answer the door.

"I just had that gong installed," said Olot. "I might have to change it before the baby is born, though. Chancy says the gong is too loud."

"She's right," said Cheeble. "My mother had fourteen kids. You don't want to wake a sleeping baby if you can avoid it."

When Chancy came back into the room, she had two ogres with her.

"Everyone, I want you to meet Twark and Skweely," said Olot. "I talked to them at Cory's party yesterday when I saw what a great job they did cleaning up the broken furniture. I offered them jobs and they accepted. They're going to help us haul our instruments around."

"New roadies!" cried Cheeble. "Great!"

"Do we really need two?" Skippy asked.

Olot nodded. "It will get us set up a lot faster if we have two. Chancy can't lift heavy things anymore and I have to handle the administrative end when we go places, so I can't do it, either. We've been getting a lot more requests since we played at those ogre parties and we keep getting more every day. Everyone, take a break. I want to show Twark and Skweely what they'll need to do."

While the other members of Zephyr went to the table to get food, Cory took the song she'd written out of her pocket. She hadn't had a chance to try the song on her drums because she kept her instruments at Olot's cave. Using a light touch, she beat out the rhythm of the song, going over the more difficult parts a couple of times. When she'd finished playing it all the way through twice, she looked up and saw that everyone was watching her.

"What was that?" asked Daisy.

Cory shrugged. "Just something I've been working on. It's not finished yet. I mean, it is, but I want to polish it a bit."

"It sounded great to me!" said Perky.

"Me, too," Cheeble announced. "Can we try it?"

"It really isn't ready yet," protested Cory.

"I liked it!" Twark said. "But it sounds kind of sad."

"It is sad," Cory told them. "Zephyr plays so many upbeat songs that I thought I'd write something really different."

"Let's see what we can do with it," said Olot. "Cory, can you teach it to us?"

"I guess," she replied. "It's called 'Lily Rose' and is about a fairy who lost her love in the Troll Wars. It starts like this."

"Do you mind if we hang around and listen?" asked Skweely.

"Go right ahead," said Olot.

The two ogres sat on the couch with Chancy while Cory sang the song through. She sang it again a second and third time until everyone had gotten it. When they knew the words, they picked up their instruments, taking their cues from Cory. They practiced the song until they all thought they had it, then played it one more time. As the last notes faded away, Cory heard loud sobbing. Twark and Skweely were both crying. Chancy was weeping into one of the pillows from the couch. Tears streamed down the faces of Skippy's two girlfriends.

"That was so sad!" cried Skweely. "I loved it!"

"I did, too!" blubbered Twark. "And I never like sad songs!"

"It was b . . . b . . . beautiful!" Chancy wailed.

"Wow!" said Cory. "I didn't know it would have such a big effect!" She turned to talk to her friends and saw that they were crying as well.

"I think we should take a break for lunch," Olot said, sniffling.

Chancy was still dabbing at her eyes, so Cory got up to help Olot. She followed him into the kitchen carrying the empty platters from the table. "That was some song you wrote," said Olot. "Ogres don't usually cry. In fact, I think that's the first time I've cried since I was a kid."

"I'm sorry," said Cory. "Maybe we shouldn't play it in public."

"Are you kidding! It was great!" Olot told her. "I can't wait to play it again. Chancy tells me that everyone needs a good cry now and then."

"After lunch, why don't we play a happy song," Cory suggested.

Olot nodded. "Like 'June Bug Jamboree.'"

By the time they carried out the sandwiches that Chancy had made earlier, everyone was looking more cheerful. "Skweely and I should go," said Twark.

"Wouldn't you like to eat first?" asked Chancy. "I made plenty of sandwiches."

"If you insist," Skweely said, going to the front of the line.

During lunch, all anyone could talk about was Cory's new song. Apparently, Cory was the only one who hadn't cried. When lunch was over, Olot asked the band members what they wanted to play next and everyone agreed that "June Bug Jamboree" was the best song to play after "Lily Rose." Twark and Skweely stayed until midafternoon.

The band went through their play list until it was almost suppertime. When Skippy said that his lips were too sore to play his pan pipes anymore, everyone agreed that rehearsal was over. Cory was covering her drums when Daisy came to see her. "I love your new song," Daisy told her. "How long did it take you to write it?"

"I've been working on it off and on for a while," said Cory. "I'm glad you like it. Tell me, what happened with you and Jonas McDonald? You said you thought he was nice."

"He was very nice, but when he kissed me, I knew he wasn't the one. There wasn't any spark between us. Do you know what I mean?"

"Yes, I do," said Cory. She definitely felt more than a spark when Blue kissed her. "Do you feel anything when you kiss Ptolomy?"

"No, not really. I mean, I thought I did at first, but then I realized that it was his lip ring digging into my lip," Daisy told her. "It doesn't matter, though. I already broke up with him."

"That was fast," Cory said.

Daisy shrugged. "Why drag it out when you know a guy isn't right for you? Someday I'll meet my true love."

"I'm sure you will," said Cory, hoping it would happen soon.

When Cory finally went outside, Macks was there, lying on the ground beside Lucille. Cory had to nudge him awake. He sat up, groggy, but he grinned when he saw Cory. "Twark and Skweely told me you came up with a great song. I can't wait to hear it."

"You've been out here that long? They left hours ago. You should have come inside to wait."

"I was fine," Macks said as he brushed a fallen leaf off Lucille's seat.

"Well, did you ask Estel to marry you? Did she say yes?" Cory asked him.

Macks grinned until his smile almost reached his ears. "I did and she did! I'm getting married!"

"Congratulations!" Cory cried. "That's wonderful news!"

"I know," said Macks. "I'll have to go tell my parents. My mother is crazy about Estel." He was helping Cory onto the solar cycle when he remembered to ask, "Am I going to hear that song tomorrow at the Battle of the Bands?"

"You will," Cory told him. "Everyone told me they want it on our list. Just be prepared to cry."

"I never cry," said Macks.

"We'll see about that," Cory murmured as she took her seat on the cycle.

They had scarcely started for home when Cory had a vision. Once again it showed two people she didn't know. Normally she would have planned to go to her office to try to find their pictures that night, but she needed to get some sleep before the Battle of the Bands. With all that she had going on, she wasn't sure when she'd get the chance to work on matches. Maybe after Micah and Quince's wedding, which was the day after the Battle of the Bands. It wasn't as if she'd forget what the people in her vision looked like. If she didn't make the match right away, she'd keep *seeing* the vision until she'd handled it.

The sun was setting when they arrived at the house, and Blue's cycle was already parked in the drive. Macks was still turning off his cycle as Laudine Kundry stepped into the front yard. When Macks saw her, he went inside, leaving Cory and Laudine to have a private conversation.

"How do you always seem to know when I get home?" Cory asked her.

"Magic," said Laudine. "Although sometimes I just look out my window. I wanted to tell you that I located Darkin Flay. He's a salesman working for a company that sells magic ingredients to witches. He goes from trade show to trade show. The next trade show in New Town will be next week. We can go together if you'd like."

"I would like that," said Cory. "A trade show for witches should be a lot of fun."

"Or very dangerous," said Laudine. "It depends on who shows up. I need to go. My supper is getting cold."

Cory was headed into the house when she heard a faint sound behind her. Thinking that Laudine had remembered something else and was coming back to see her again, she turned around, but there was no sign of her neighbor. A moment later, Weegie came running out of the underbrush.

"Did you see him?" the woodchuck asked her. "The man who's been lurking around the yard was just here. I bit his leg, which tasted really bad."

Cory shook her head. "I didn't see anyone."

"Well, he was weird. And the weirdest thing about him was that when I bit him, he didn't even seem to feel it."

CHAPTER

7

The Battle of the Bands was held beside Turquoise Lake, the same place where Cory and Blue had gone to see the nymphs perform *Swan Lake* and Rina had caused an accident. It was the largest park in the area and ideal for the expected crowd. When the members of Zephyr arrived, a huge crowd had already assembled. There were three platforms set up in front of the lake; Cory could see her drums set up on the center stage.

When Cory reached the stage with Blue and Macks, Olot came over to see them. "Twark, Skweely, and I got here a couple of hours ago. Jack Horner had the bands pull straws to see where to set up. I got the middle-size straw, so we got the second stage. I supervised setup, but Twark and Skweely are going to work out just fine as roadies. They did a good job and didn't need much direction."

"What do you know about the other bands?" asked Blue.

Olot turned to point at the first stage, where three ogres and two ogresses were dressed in old-fashioned hides. "That group is called Boulder of Ages. They dress like ogres used to, but they play heavy rock."

"I know the big ogre with the tuft of hair," said Blue. "That's Sidnee. We were in band together in Junior Fey School. He's a great guy."

Olot turned to face the other way. "The fairies and elves climbing on the third stage make up the band '2 by 2.' There are two sets of fairy twins and two sets of elf twins in the group. They play folk music."

"Shouldn't they be called 2 by 2 by 2 by 2 since there are four sets of twins?" Macks said with a laugh.

"Yeah, really!" Cheeble said as he came up to listen to Olot. "Did Jack tell you about the rules?"

Olot nodded. "We'll be playing three songs. Each band will play one, then it's the next band's turn. If there's a tie, the two tied bands will play one more song each."

The other members of Zephyr had gathered around. "What songs are we going to play?" Daisy asked.

"I thought we'd start with 'Morning Mist,' then 'Lily Rose' and 'June Bug Jamboree.' If there's a tie, we should play 'Summer Heat,'" said Olot.

"Oh, no," said Daisy. "We should play 'Lily Rose' last. It's so beautiful and I think we should end with that."

"I agree," Chancy declared. "I still cry when I think about that song. Put it at the end."

"You mean the third song?" said Olot. "Why do you want everyone to cry at the end?"

"Not the third song. The tie-breaker song. Even if there isn't a tie, you should play it after everyone else has finished," one of Skippy's girlfriends said. "It will make them remember it even more, and it's so beautiful."

"Is that what everyone wants?" asked Olot. When no one disagreed, he nodded. "Then 'Lily Rose' will be our tiebreaker, even if we don't need one."

"I believe it's time to warm up," said Perky. "Everyone else is getting started."

Blue and Macks left the stage while Cory hurried to her drums. Picking up her sticks, she did a warm-up exercise until Jack Horner climbed onto the first stage. The noise didn't die down until he held a horn to his lips and said, "Quiet, please!" The horn amplified his voice so that it was even louder than the ogres in the audience and everyone could hear him.

"I have got to get one of those horns," Cory heard Cheeble mutter.

"Welcome to the Battle of the Bands!" Jack Horner announced. "We have three bands with us today. Boulder of Ages," he said, pointing at the ogre band. "Zephyr, and 2 by 2!" He pointed to the others in turn.

The noise was deafening as the audience screamed and shouted, and the ogres in the crowd roared.

"The rules of the Battle are as follows," Jack said when the noise had died down again. "Each band will play three songs. The audience will judge the bands' performances and show how much they liked them with their applause. The band with the most applause will win. If there is a tie, the tied bands will play one more song. The winning band will receive the title of Best Band, a gift card for Jack Horner's restaurants for each band member, and a recording contract with Abracadabra Music. And now, let's all listen to Boulder of Ages play their first song, 'The Boulder I Get, The More I Love You'!"

The audience applauded again as the band began to play, but the music quickly drowned out everything else. The ogres' song started out loud and got louder. Instead of traditional instruments, they banged rocks together, pulled the tails of cats so they'd screech, broke boards over one another's heads, and screamed the words to the song, most of which Cory couldn't make out. They were so loud that Cory felt sorry for the people directly in front of the stage.

After watching the band in disbelief for most of the song, Cory turned to look out over the audience. The ogres among the crowd were going crazy, but most of the other beings there had their fingers in their ears. When the song ended, they actually looked relieved.

Jack Horner jumped onto Zephyr's stage and held up his hand. As the audience grew quiet, he said, "And now we're going to hear Zephyr playing . . ."—he turned to Olot, who whispered in his ear. " 'Morning Mist'!" Jack repeated through the horn.

"Boo! Boo!" cried some fairies in the audience, but the cheering soon drowned them out. Cory noticed that a few fairies were giving her dirty looks. Apparently, some of the guild members who were still mad at her had come to the concert. It bothered her until she started to lay down the beat for the song, and then she forgot all about them.

Although "Morning Mist" was a quiet song, it soon drew everyone in. The spirits of the fey are in tune with nature, and they felt it as they heard the sounds of a day just beginning. When the song was over, even the fairies looked contented. The applause was just as loud as it had been after Boulder of Ages played.

When Cory put down her drumsticks, Jack Horner was already standing on 2 by 2's stage. "And now, 2 by 2 playing 'C U 2morrow.'"

Cory watched, interested, as the fairies and elves began to play. She counted two sets of pan pipes, one set of wind chimes, one long, curled horn, a tiny hand drum, a fiddle, and two members who did nothing but sing. The music was soft and sweet, but didn't carry well enough for her to make out the words.

Although the fairies and elves in the audience seemed to enjoy 2 by 2's music, the ogres quickly got bored and started talking to one another. A fight broke out when some elves tried to shush their noisier neighbors. When a fairy punched an ogre in the nose, the ogre picked up the fairy and hurled him toward the lake. The fairy would have ended up in the water if he hadn't turned small and sprouted wings. Two FLEA officers forced their way through the crowd to break up the fight that was starting to spread. People hardly noticed when 2 by 2 finished their song. Only the fairies and elves who weren't fighting applauded.

When Boulder of Ages started their next song, "You're the Pebble in My Shoe," Cory thought it sounded just like their first. As far as she could tell, the only difference was that they had howling wolves instead of screeching cats. The ogres in the audience seemed to like it just as much.

"June Bug Jamboree" got the audience involved the way it always did. Ogres swatted at the june bugs that weren't really there, while the rest of the audience either acted like they saw the bugs, or ducked to avoid the ogres' meaty hands. Cory no longer saw any fairies glaring at her.

When 2 by 2 played their second song, "2 Late 4 Love," the fairies and elves tried to listen, but the ogres started shouting until no one could hear the band at all.

"Get 'em off the stage!" shouted one ogre.

"They stink!" screamed another.

Cory wasn't sure when the band's song ended.

The only instruments that Boulder of Ages used in their third song, "Stone Dust," were rocks. They smashed rocks with other rocks, pounded rocks with rocks, and slammed rocks onto the wooden stage, splintering the floor. Cory thought they sounded like workers in a quarry, but the ogres in the audience seemed to love it. When one of the band members fell into the hole he'd made in the stage, Cory thought they might stop playing. They didn't, though, and the ogre climbed out and started throwing rocks at his bandmates. The ogres in the audience went insane.

It was Zephyr's turn to play next. They started playing "Summer Heat" and the audience became quiet, acting as if they actually felt the heat of the sun, the dry grass beneath their feet, and the cool water of the stream. As the song ended, there was a loud sigh as if from every throat. Suddenly, the crowd went wild, from the most delicate fairy to the toughest ogre and everyone in between.

Cory glanced at her bandmates and saw the pleased looks on their faces. *We've got this*, she thought.

And then it was time for 2 by 2's third song. It was called "2 Day + 2 Night = 4 Ever." The band members looked nervous when they started to play. As soon as the ogres began to shout, the twins all grabbed their instruments and left the stage.

Jack jumped onto the abandoned stage and held the horn to his lips. "I guess that leaves us with two choices for Best Band. Let's hear it for Boulder of Ages!"

The ogres clapped, cheered, and roared, but nobody else did.

"Now tell me what you think of Zephyr!" shouted Jack.

Everyone cheered and clapped, including the members of Boulder of Ages. The ogres roared even louder than before.

"I think we have our winner!" cried Jack. "I now proclaim that the title of Best Band goes to Zephyr!"

Cory and all her bandmates grinned. She spotted Blue in the audience and saw that his smile was even broader than her own.

The crowd was screaming when Olot took the horn from Jack. As soon as Olot started talking, the audience became silent. "My band and I would like to play one more song, if that's all right with you."

The crowd screamed until Olot held up his hand. "The name of the song is 'Lily Rose' and it was written by Cory Feathering."

Handing the horn to Jack, Olot picked up his lute and waited for Cory to start. By the time the rest of the band joined in, she was already lost in the music. People in the audience began to cry after the first few stanzas. Within minutes, tears glistened in everyone's eyes. When the song was over, Cory finally looked up. She felt awful at first; fairies, ogres, elves, satyrs, nymphs, humans, and every other kind of being that was there was crying. Tears flowed, people wailed or sobbed. But it wasn't until they turned to one another and began crying in each other's arms that Cory knew what was really happening. They weren't just feeling sad, they were feeling the loss of a great love, the way Lily Rose did in the song.

Cory turned to her friends in the band who were crying just as much as the people in the audience. "Should we play a happier song now?" she asked.

"No," said Cheeble, who was standing closest to her. "Let's leave it with that." Taking a handkerchief out of his pocket, he blew his nose, then gave her a watery smile. "That song was perfect."

When the cheering started, Cory thought she might go deaf. People cheered even as they wiped tears from their eyes. Ogres and fairies who had been fighting only a short time before were standing there with their arms around each other, and they were all cheering for her song.

Cory had never felt so proud.

After Jack presented Olot with a plaque for Best Band and gave him the gift cards and the information for Abracadabra Music, the crowd cheered again. When it was finally time to go, and the crowd was leaving, Blue joined Cory on the stage. Twark and Skweely were both red-eyed when they started to pack up the instruments.

"That was fantastic!" Blue said as he picked up Cory and spun her around. "You have an amazing talent!"

She laughed and kissed him back when he kissed her. "I guess the song struck a note with a lot of people," she said when he set her down.

"With everyone!" said Blue. "I even saw the FLEA officers crying. I didn't know that some of them had tear ducts."

Cory glanced at the members of the audience who were trailing behind. She saw ogres talking to fairies, she saw FLEA officers wiping their eyes, and she saw Macks and Estel in a passionate embrace.

"When we get married, you aren't going to want a traditional ogre wedding, are you?" she asked Blue.

"No," he said. "My parents didn't even have a traditional ogre wedding."

"Good," said Cory, relieved.

Cory felt as if she were floating for the rest of the day. Creampuff prepared a big celebratory supper, and her grandfather toasted her with apple wine. "To my granddaughter, who has more talents than I ever imagined!" he said.

"Thank you, Grandfather," Cory told him. "I wasn't the only one who played, though. Everyone in Zephyr deserves the credit."

"Yes, but it was your song that everyone is still talking about," said Blue. "It was amazing."

"You're both biased," Cory said with a laugh.

"Of course, but it's also true," Blue replied.

After a long and stressful day, Cory went to bed still excited and unsure if she'd be able to go to sleep. She was lying in bed, reading a book she'd borrowed from her grandfather, when she heard scratching on her balcony door. Jumping out of bed, she opened the door and let Shimmer into the room. The little dragon flew onto the bed and curled up in the middle, then promptly fell asleep. Cory had to push Shimmer to one side to make room for herself. Climbing back into bed, she read another chapter and was about to turn out the light when she heard another sound outside. Shimmer must have heard it, too, because she got up suddenly and flew to the door, crying until Cory opened it.

Certain that they must have heard some sort of animal, Cory waited for the little dragon to return. When time passed and she didn't come back, Cory pulled on her robe and went downstairs to knock on Blue's door.

"I think there might be something outside," she told him when he opened the door. "Shimmer went to investigate and hasn't come back."

"Just a moment," he said, and shut the door. He was back out a little while later wearing his robe over his pajamas and shoes on his feet.

"Is everything all right?" Macks asked from two doors down.

"We're going to see what Shimmer found outside," Blue told him.

Macks grabbed his shoes and followed them down the hall. They went out the back door onto the terrace and stopped to look around. There was a full moon, and everything stood out in an eerie light.

"Is that fire coming out of Shimmer's den?" Blue asked, peering into the darkness.

Cory looked toward the den and saw a bright glow on the ground outside the opening. She jumped when she heard a horrible bellow and the glow flashed brighter. All three of them began to run.

"Shimmer! Are you all right?" Cory called.

Blue reached the den first. He stopped just outside the opening. Macks stopped beside him and said, "Who is that?"

Shimmer was standing a few feet inside her den with her back to the opening. A being as tall as an ogre faced her from the other end of the cave. Big and broad-chested, he had a blocky head and knobs sticking out from either side of his neck. When he saw Cory, he let out a half-hearted roar.

Taking it as a challenge, Macks roared back. The full-blooded ogre's roar was enough to make the walls of the den shake. The creature cowered as if someone had hit him.

"May I ask what you're doing in my dragon's den?" asked Cory.

"Hiding, until I could jump out and scare you. At least that was my assignment. But when I got here and saw that you hang out with ogres, I figured you wouldn't find me all that scary."

"Are you a member of the Itinerant Troublemakers Guild?" asked Blue. "Because if you are, I need your name and membership ID number. I'm FLEA Officer Blue."

"This just keeps getting better and better," the being said. "And I was told this would be an easy assignment! Technically my name is Frankenstein's Monster, although I prefer Frankenstein. I have my guild ID card here somewhere." He started patting his pockets. "I was supposed to be here a few weeks ago, but my last job terrorizing villagers in the mountains ran a little long."

"You shouldn't be here at all now," said Macks. "The ITG contracts on scaring Cory were all canceled when the guilds that placed them lost the court case."

"You have got to be kidding me! I've been hanging out here, trying to figure out how to do my job for days now and the contract was canceled? No one told me! I've got to talk to somebody in the main office. I have three other villages I'm supposed to visit back in the mountains, but I came here instead. I can't believe the guild loused up my schedule like this! I'm not the only one, either. Wolfie's going to be mad when he hears that he didn't need to come to town."

"Who is Wolfie?" asked Blue.

"A friend of mine. If you'll call off your dragon, you can talk to him yourself. No more fire, okay? I *really* hate fire."

"Come here, Shimmer," Cory called. The little dragon turned and ran to her, flying into Cory's arms with one beat of her wings.

"If I'd known there was a dragon here, I never would have taken this job," Frankenstein muttered as he stomped out of the cave.

Cory rubbed her nose as he passed her. Frankenstein smelled awful! "He must be the one Weegie was telling me about," she told Blue.

When Frankenstein was well outside the den, he opened his mouth and howled three times. He was about to howl again when something moved among the trees and a werewolf slunk into the moonlight. "That's enough already! I heard you the first time!" said the werewolf.

"We don't have to hide anymore," Frankenstein told his friend.

"I wasn't hiding! I was waiting for the full moon to come out. It makes a bigger impression when I do this." Positioning himself so that he stood with the moon behind him, the werewolf threw back his head and howled.

Even though Cory could see the source of the sound, she shivered and grabbed hold of Blue's hand.

"You're right," said Macks. "That was very impressive."

"So why did you call me?" Wolfie asked Frankenstein.

"The contract was canceled and the main office didn't tell us! We came here for nothing!" the monster said.

"Is that so? Well, if that's the case, I'm going home. If I lope fast enough, I should be home before dawn. See you later, Frankie!" the werewolf said, and disappeared into the darkness.

"Not if I see you first!" Frankenstein called after him.

"About that guild ID card . . . ," said Blue.

"I swear I've got it here somewhere," the monster said, patting his pockets again.

"Don't worry about it," Blue told him. "Just go and don't ever come back."

"With pleasure!" Frankenstein said. With a wave of his hand, he tromped off into the darkness, leaving nothing but a lingering odor behind.

"I hope that was the last of the ITG members coming after me," Cory said with a yawn.

"So do I," said Blue. "You don't deserve to be harassed."

"I was more concerned about getting some sleep. No maid of honor wants to look like something the monster dragged in."

This time when Cory crawled back into bed, she fell asleep right away. Shimmer had stayed outside, so

Cory was confused when something in the room woke her a few hours later. She looked around, wondering what had woken her, when she spotted a vague shape at the foot of her bed. Cory peered at the figure, which seemed to be reaching toward her.

"Lorelie . . . ," the figure moaned.

"Who is Lorelie?" Cory asked as she sat up. She turned on the fairy light beside her bed and realized that she could see through whatever was standing there.

"Turn that off!" the creature ordered.

"You're a ghost, aren't you?" said Cory. "Do you want the light off because you think you'll be scarier?"

"No! I want it off because I've been in the dark all night and the bright light coming on like that hurts my eyes. Turn it off, will you?"

Cory sighed and turned off the light. "You didn't answer my question. Who is Lorelie?"

"You are, of course," said the ghost.

"No, I'm not," replied Cory. "There is no Lorelie in this house."

There was a rustling sound as the ghost riffled through a small stack of leaves. "Are you Chloe? Winnie? Francine? Cory?"

"Yep, I'm that last one. I'm Cory."

"Dang! I must have gotten my leaves mixed up again. You were supposed to be my last visit of the night. Oh, well. At least I found the right house." The leaves vanished as the ghost began to moan, "Cory . . ."

"Are you a member of the ITG?" Cory asked. "Because if you are, you shouldn't have come. The contracts to harass me have been canceled."

"Nope. No connection," said the ghost. "Cory . . ."

The door to the room suddenly burst open and three putti ran in brandishing squirt guns. "I told you I smelled a ghost!" cried the chef, Creampuff. "I have the best sniffer in the house!"

"You can smell ghosts?" Cory asked, even as the ghost floated away from the putti, moaning.

"Putti have amazing sniffers," Orville said, touching his nose.

"Stay away from me!" cried the ghost.

"Ghosts don't like us because we're one of the few beings that can sense them," said Orville.

"Us and cats," Creampuff told Cory.

"Leave me alone!" the ghost wailed. "I have a job to do."

"Not in this house!" said Orville. "Get out and don't come back!"

All three putti started shooting their squirt guns at the ghost. Shrieking, it fled through the outside wall.

"Thanks for that," Cory told the putti. "I'm curious, though. What do ghosts smell like?"

"Freezer-burned bananas," said Creampuff.

"What's in the squirt guns?"

"Lemon juice," Orville declared. "Ghosts can't abide anything citrus. Why don't you keep this one? You never know when you might need it. I'll put it in here." Walking around Cory's bed, he tucked it in her night-stand drawer.

"You learn something new every day. Thanks again for your help," she said, lying down. "But I really need to get some rest."

"Good night, miss," Orville said, and hustled the other putti from the room.

Cory was just drifting off when it occurred to her that she had no idea why the ghost had been there. *If only the putti hadn't come in quite so soon,* she thought before she fell asleep.

CHAPTER

8

The next morning, Cory and Blue rode with Lionel, Macks, and Estel to the park where Micah and Quince's wedding was being held. After parking the car, they started following signs that read, THIS WAY TO THE WEDDING! Cory carried the bag with her new shoes and the things she was going to need to get ready. She was hoping she hadn't forgotten anything when Blue said, "There are the tents." She looked up to see two white tents set up in a small clearing.

"They aren't very big," remarked Macks. "It must be a small wedding."

"I want a huge wedding, Macksie," said Estel.

"I know, sweetums, and that's what we'll have," Macks told her.

"Creampuff was disappointed that she wasn't going to have to cook for a lot of people," Lionel said.

"They didn't invite very many—only family and close friends," said Cory. "Look, there are my grandparents."

Clayton and Deidre Fleuren stood at the edge of a small crowd, looking lost and slightly confused. They waved when they spotted Cory and Blue.

"Why are you wearing that?" Deidre said, wrinkling her nose at Cory's ordinary clothes. "I thought you were supposed to be in this wedding."

"I am," Cory replied, and held up the bag she was carrying. "The store is bringing the dresses here. I have to go change my clothes."

"I don't know if Quince is here," said Deidre. "Micah said he hasn't seen her."

"That's a good thing," Cory told her. "It's supposed to be bad luck for the groom to see the bride the day of the wedding. At least not until she walks down the aisle. Is her family here?"

"I don't know!" Deidre snapped. "No one has introduced me to anyone. Hello, Lionel. I wasn't expecting to see you. I thought you were dead."

"No, I'm still very much alive," Lionel said with a laugh.

"It's good to see you again," Cory's other grandfather, Clayton, said as he held out his hand.

"Cory," Deidre said in a loud whisper. "Why did you bring two ogres with you? I told you they're nothing but trouble."

Cory glanced at Macks. He looked particularly rough with his broken nose and missing tooth, but at least he was wearing a nice suit. "Macks is our friend, Grandmother. He's also a friend of Micah's. And this is Macks's fiancée, Estel."

"Well, I never!" said Deidre.

"Your mother hasn't arrived yet," said Clayton. "I thought she'd be here."

"I'm sure she was invited," Cory said as she looked around. "I bet she shows up at the last minute."

"She'd better hurry, then," Blue told her. "The wedding is supposed to start soon."

"I need to go find Quince and get ready. I'll see you at the reception," Cory said, and kissed Blue.

Cory wasn't sure where to look. She peeked into both tents. A long buffet table was set up in the first tent, along with smaller tables and lots of chairs, but there was no one in it. Everyone seemed to be headed for the second tent. When she peeked inside, she saw that rows of chairs had been set up to face the other end. Micah's neighbors Salazar, Felice, Selene, and Wanita were seated together on one side. She also saw a few teachers who taught with Micah, as well as some people she didn't know.

Cory finally looked past the two tents and saw a third that was much smaller. She had taken a few steps toward it when she heard Quince wail, "What am I going to do?"

"How could this have happened?" cried a woman's voice.

"What's wrong?" Cory asked as she stepped into the tent.

Quince was sitting on a chair holding a garish pink dress covered with ruffles. Another dress in a sickly shade of green was hanging from the corner of a large mirror. A woman who looked like an older version of Quince stood beside her, wringing her hands.

"Oh, Cory, I don't know what to do," Quince said, holding up the pink dress. "They delivered this instead of the dress I ordered. Look at the color! Look at the size! And the ruffles! I can't wear this."

"And that dress is for you," the woman said, pointing at the one hanging on the mirror.

"I'm sorry that I forgot to introduce you, Cory. This is my mother, May Apple," said Quince.

"Everyone calls me May," the woman told her.

"It's nice to meet you," Cory said, then turned to look at the dresses. She was afraid that fairies were trying to ruin the wedding just because she was involved, and was thinking that she never should have agreed to be Quince's maid of honor, when it suddenly occurred to her that the dresses seemed very familiar. Surely she had seen them before. Cory was trying to remember their visit to the store, when she recalled where she had seen the dresses. "These are the gowns those ogresses picked out! They must have gotten the tags mixed up. I bet those sprite children switched the tags! It's just the kind of thing sprites like to do."

"But what am I going to wear?" Quince cried. "The ceremony is going to start soon and no one would even see me in this dress."

"Can we send someone to the store to get the right ones?" asked Cory.

Quince shook her head. "There isn't time."

"Even if we could stand the color, we can't alter them. There's far too much fabric to pin up," said Quince's mother.

Cory thought for a moment. If they couldn't exchange the dresses, or pin them up, maybe there was something else they could do—something that wouldn't take any time at all. "Just a minute," she said. "I might know someone who can help."

Cory ran to the tent where the ceremony was about to begin. Spotting Micah's neighbors, she darted to the row where Wanita was seated. "Can you come with me?" she asked the witch.

"I don't want to miss the start of the wedding," said Wanita. "I do love watching the bride walk down the aisle. I always watch to see if she'll trip."

"Believe me, you won't miss a thing," Cory told her.

When Wanita stood up, Cory hustled her out of the tent. "We need your help," she said, leading her straight to Quince. "The store brought the wrong dresses."

"What do you want me to do—turn the shop girl into a mackerel?" asked Wanita.

"Quince, do you remember Wanita? You may have met at my birthday party," Cory said. When Quince nodded, Cory turned back to Wanita. "Actually, I was hoping you could change the dresses. These were made for ogresses. They aren't anything like the dresses we ordered."

"I see!" Wanita said when Quince held up her dress. "You want me to make them smaller."

"And less pink," said Quince. "And lose the ruffles. I want the dress I picked out—not this!"

Wanita shrugged. "I can do that. But first you have to put them on. It'll be a lot easier to get the right sizes if you're wearing them."

As Cory and Quince changed their clothes, May looked at Wanita and said, "You can do all this in just a few minutes?"

"I'm a witch. I can do lots of things in a few minutes. Tsk! This is taking too long. I want to get back to the tent to make sure no one takes my seat. Here, let me help."

With a wave of her hand and a few mumbled words, Cory and Quince were wearing the dresses.

"Oh!" Quince cried out from inside the enormous pink pile of fabric where only the top of her head was visible.

Cory struggled inside the green dress, trying to pull the neckline below her eyes so she could see.

"All right!" said Wanita. "Size first!" With a wave of her hand, the dresses shrank until they fit the girls.

"And next we'll lose the ruffles!"

The ruffles vanished, leaving two plain, but full-skirted dresses.

"Can you change the—" Quince began.

"Style? Of course! We'll start with the bride's. The neckline is all wrong. No, not that. Maybe this. A little low. No, not low enough. Go stand in front of the mirror and tell me when I hit on something that you like. Sleeves? Short sleeves? No sleeves? High waist? Low waist? No waist? Long train, no train?"

Cory and May stood back to watch as the gown changed on Quince with every flick of Wanita's wrist. When Quince finally liked the style, Wanita said, "Now about the color. Are you sure you want to change it? I actually like the pink."

"But I don't," Quince said firmly. "I want it to be a very pale blue."

It took three tries before Wanita hit on a color that Quince liked. Then it was Cory's turn. Instead of letting the witch try her hit-and-miss approach, she told Wanita what she wanted. It took her just a few tries to get the dress close to the one Cory had originally picked out.

"Can I go now?" Wanita asked when Quince and Cory were satisfied.

"Yes, and thank you very much!" Quince told her.

"You're welcome," said Wanita. "We can call this my wedding present to you and Micah. I bought you some dishes and wrapped them myself. They're already on your gift table, but I think I'll take them back and keep them now. I really like their pig pattern, and apparently I like pink a lot more than you do."

"I should go sit down now, too," May said as Wanita ran out of the tent. "You girls both look lovely!"

And then she was gone, leaving the girls to pick up their bouquets. "What do you think the ogresses are going to do when they end up with our dresses?" Cory asked Quince as they left the tent.

"I can only imagine!" Quince said, and started to giggle. She was still grinning when the music started and Cory preceded her into the bigger tent.

A single fiddler was playing just inside the opening. Cory glanced at him as she passed by and nearly tripped over her own feet. It was one of the twins from the Battle of the Bands, and the sour look he gave her was enough to curdle milk. The music faltered for a second, picking up again a moment later. Cory kept walking, focusing on the people on either side of the aisle.

Her smile grew broader when she spotted Blue sitting between Lionel and Macks, right behind her mother's parents. Micah was only a few paces beyond, but the only one he was looking at was Quince. Cory recognized the man standing beside him. It was Mr. Chirith, a teacher from the Junior Fey School. The man standing in front of him was Judge Terwilliger, one of Micah's old students.

As Quince approached Micah, Cory stepped to the side. Cory glanced over her shoulder when the judge started talking. There weren't that many people there, so it was easy to see that her mother hadn't shown up. Cory was still looking behind her when six tiny fairies dressed in pink and yellow flew into the tent and down the aisle. They were carrying baskets full of flower petals to sprinkle on the heads of the guests. When their baskets were empty, they left and came back with more petals, dumping them on Quince and Micah. Quince started to sneeze, and Micah looked alarmed. Judge Terwilliger didn't seem to notice and kept talking, even though Micah kept shooting the fairies annoyed looks.

Cory wondered if the fairies were there to cause trouble because of her. If this was her fault, shouldn't she do something to stop them? Unable to think of anything she could do without wrecking the wedding, she stood there, watching helplessly as the fairies came back again.

"You may kiss the bride," Judge Terwilliger announced, and Cory realized that she had missed most of what he'd said.

Micah turned to kiss Quince, and Cory could see how happy they were. It made her feel pleased with herself to know that she was the one who had brought them together.

The music started again, and the newlyweds had just begun to walk down the aisle when the tiny fairies returned, their baskets filled with petals mixed with glitter. They scattered the sparkling petals on the bride, the groom, and everyone near the aisle. Quince sneezed again, and this time she couldn't seem to stop. Hiking up her skirts with one hand, she hurried out of the tent with Micah running to keep up and the fiddler playing faster to match her pace.

"Well, that was different," said the judge, loud enough so only the people near him could hear.

Cory and Mr. Chirith walked down the aisle side by side. Everyone was going into the next tent, where the tables and chairs were set up, but Cory stepped aside to wait for Blue.

"You look beautiful!" he said when he saw her.

"Thank you," Cory told him. "You wouldn't believe what we had to go through for our dresses."

"Was there a problem? I heard that you came for Wanita."

"There was, but it wasn't anything we couldn't handle. I'll tell you all about it later."

"Hey, Cory! You've gotta come try the food!" Macks called to her. "Creampuff outdid herself this time!"

"Shall we join him?" Cory asked Blue. He chuckled and nodded, so she took his hand and they started for the buffet table. They were almost there when Cory got sidetracked by Quince's angry voice. She spotted the bride standing in the corner, talking to a fairy dressed all in yellow.

"I don't know why you didn't ask me first!" Quince was saying to the fairy. Although the fairy was full-size, Cory recognized her as one of the tiny fairies that had scattered flower petals during the ceremony.

"It was our surprise wedding gift to you! It wouldn't have been a surprise if we'd told you. Some people are so unappreciative!" the fairy cried before flouncing off.

"Why don't you join Macks?" Cory said to Blue. "I'll be back in just a minute."

"Is everything all right?" she asked Quince, who was wiping her nose with a handkerchief.

Quince glanced at her, then steered her away from the other guests. "The fairies who dropped the flower petals during the ceremony are my cousins. They know I'm allergic to flowers, but they did it anyway. I suppose it's possible they forgot about my allergy, but even so, they should have asked. It was my wedding, after all."

"I didn't know that you're allergic to flowers," said Cory.

Quince nodded. "It's a shameful secret to have when you come from a family of flower fairies. It's why I didn't go into the family business."

"And it's why you wanted artificial flowers for the bouquets!" said Cory. "I don't think it's anything to be ashamed of, but I won't tell anyone."

"I knew I could count on you!" Quince replied. "Micah told me that you never tell anyone's secrets. Excuse me, there he is. I need to talk to him."

Cory was on her way back to the buffet table when she saw Deidre talking to the genie Salazar. "That's so interesting!" Cory's grandmother exclaimed. "Tell me, what was the strangest thing that any of your clients has ever wished for?"

"Usually it's power or riches. Love is a big one, too, but we can't make people fall in love. I'd have to say that the strangest requests are when someone makes a wish without really thinking about it. I had one person ask for a gumball machine. And another wished the day was over so she could put her children to bed."

"What a waste of a good wish!" Deidre cried. "What would you have wished for if you could have wished for anything?"

"More vacations!" said Salazar.

Cory laughed and kept walking until Wanita called out to her. "Cory, you never told me that your grandfather is *the* Clayton Fleuren, who creates those wonderful fish-scale models! I love your work, Mr. Fleuren. I saw a model you did of a pig at the Porcine Palace, where I take Theo for grooming. It was in a glass case, but it looked so real I thought it might be alive."

"I'm glad you like my models," said Cory's grandfather. "I made that pig model years ago. I remember it very well because I had such a hard time finding fish with the exact shade of pink scales that I needed."

"You should have seen the model Grandfather made of Prince Rupert's castle," Cory told Wanita.

"I would have loved to have seen that!" Wanita cried as Cory turned toward the food table again. "What are you working on now?"

When Cory finally got in line, she was behind the twins, Selene and Felice, who were talking to one of their old teachers, Mr. Chirith.

"We remember you better than any of our other teachers," Selene was telling him.

Felice nodded. "You had a major impact on our lives."

"I'm glad to hear that," he said, smiling politely. "I was afraid you might be angry after I flunked you in Shape-shifting 1. I'm glad you recognized that you both needed another year of practice before you moved on."

"We were slow at developing our abilities," Felice admitted. "There was one thing you did that we had a terrible time mastering. Would you mind showing us again how you do the blink and change?"

"Right now?" he said. "I wouldn't mind showing you, but I don't think this is either the time or the place."

"I told you he's getting too old to do it," Selene told her sister. "We'll have to ask someone younger to show us."

"I suppose I could show you now," said Mr. Chirith. "Watch closely."

Felice and Selene weren't the only ones watching when the teacher's face became impassive. He blinked and an instant later, a raccoon was standing next to the table.

"That was fast," said Selene. "But we're even faster."

In a flash, the twins were leopards: one black and one spotted. With a snarl that made everyone turn and look, they sprang at the raccoon, who shot between them and ran out the opening of the tent into the forest beyond. The two leopards ran after him and were soon out of sight.

"I guess they never really did forgive him," said Deidre, who had come up behind Cory. "Oh, dear, I think one of the twins must have spilled her drink on you when she changed. If you can go take that dress off, you can probably clean it before the stain sets."

Cory glanced down. It looked as if an entire cup of berry juice had splashed on her dress. If she was going to keep it from staining, she'd have to clean it soon.

"Please tell Blue that I'll be right back," she told her grandmother, and hurried out of the tent. The little tent where she'd left her other clothes was only a few yards away. She'd change into the clothes she'd worn to the park, then . . .

Shadowy figures stepped out from behind a tree. One shoved a cloth soaked in something stinky under Cory's nose, while another held her as she struggled. She was losing consciousness when one of them slipped a bag over her head and she collapsed into the other's arms.

CHAPTER
9

Cory's head hurt when she woke. Even before she opened her eyes, she knew she was someplace unfamiliar. There was a damp, musty smell to the air, and she could hear water dripping somewhere close by. It felt as if she was lying on some kind of fur with another fur on top of her, which might have been the reason for the smell. Her thoughts faded in and out. When she was more lucid, she wondered which guild had sent people to kidnap her.

Cory finally opened her eyes, but the space was so dark that she couldn't see a thing. She tried to sit up, and groaned. Movement made her headache worse.

"She's awake!" shouted a voice.

Although she couldn't see them, she could hear people moving around her. She moaned again when someone rolled her on her side, and kept rolling her until she was wrapped so tightly that she couldn't have moved if she'd wanted to. Strong arms picked her up. She bounced with every step as they carried her through the dark. Apparently, her captors didn't need light to see. After what seemed like a long time but might have been only a few minutes, they stopped walking to bang on what sounded like a wooden door three times, then three more times. When the door opened, they carried Cory into a space just as dark as the one she'd left.

"Here you go," said a gruff voice. "Have fun!"

For some reason, that prompted laughter among her captors as they dumped her on the floor and walked out, closing the door behind them. Cory lay there, still muzzy-headed, while someone came over and poked her in the side. When Cory groaned, the person came closer. "Are you all right?" said a decidedly female voice.

"I think so," said Cory. "Unless it's not really dark in here and I've suddenly gone blind."

"Just a minute," said the voice.

Cory listened to the slap of bare feet on stone, then a door opened, flooding the space with light. She squeezed her eyes shut against the sudden glare. When she opened them again, a figure was coming toward her through the light.

"Come on, get up. The men have gone, so you don't have to stay in the dark any longer. Here, let me help you."

Cory was just starting to make out a female face when the woman pushed her hard enough that she rolled over and over, unwrapping herself. As her headache suddenly grew worse, Cory caught her breath.

"There you go," said the voice. Cory looked up and saw a female goblin gazing down at her. The goblin had silver hair, a long narrow nose, ears that hung down past her jaw, and very pretty cornflower-blue eyes. "They're waiting for me to take you to them. Come along. We have lots to do."

"Who are you? Why did you kidnap me? Where are you taking me?" Cory asked as the goblin woman helped her to her feet. She didn't realize how short the goblin was until they were standing side by side. Although Cory wasn't very tall herself, the goblin was at least a foot shorter.

"She'll answer all your questions when you see her," the woman said.

"Who is 'she'?" asked Cory, but her escort only smiled.

Cory walked on wobbly legs into the light and found that she was in a corridor with doors on both sides. When she glanced down, she noticed the red stain on the bridesmaid's dress, and for a moment thought that it was blood. She was relieved to remember that it was berry juice, and sorry that the stain was probably permanent, unless, of course, she asked a witch for help. But considering where she was, a stain on a dress was the least of her worries.

When Cory looked up again, the goblin woman was opening a door and ushering her inside. The room they entered was bright and cheery with low tables and long, low couches. Brightly colored pillows were strewn across the couches and heaped on the floor. Pierced lanterns in jewel tones of red, yellow, blue, and green hung from the ceiling, casting light on the gathered goblin women who looked up at Cory and smiled. Cory was so busy looking at everything and everyone in the room that she almost didn't notice her mother. She was seated on a couch with goblin women all around her, and they were all dressed in simple, brightly colored dresses.

"Mother? What are you doing here? Where are we?" asked Cory.

"Hurry up and tell her, Delphinium, or I will," said a quarrelsome-sounding voice. Cory turned and saw Deidre sitting on another couch.

"I was just about to, Mother," said Delphinium. "Cory, I told you that I was having a traditional goblin wedding ceremony. It's your own fault if you were taken by surprise. If you'd done a little research, you'd know that part of a goblin wedding ceremony is the kidnapping of the female blood relatives of the bride. You'll stay here until the ceremony itself, which is the day after tomorrow. You'll need to participate in certain pre-ceremony rituals, as will you, Mother."

"Huh," said Deidre. "At least you didn't knock me out and drag me here with a bag on my head."

"Did you know about this before Micah's wedding?" Cory asked her grandmother, aghast.

"I didn't have a clue until I was on my way home and some goblins made me get in a very nice solar car," said Deidre. "The windows were dark and I thought it was your grandfather Lionel's, until I got in."

"This is awful!" Cory cried. "Who would think of doing such a thing?"

"Actually, we would," said the older goblin woman seated beside Delphinium. Her dark hair, streaked with gray, was pulled back in a tight bun and she had a single eyebrow that stretched from one side of her face to the other. "Kidnapping the members of the wedding party is a time-honored tradition among goblin-kind. Your mother is marrying into one of the most respected goblin families—mine. We expect her to follow all of our traditions. We expect you to as well."

"Cory, this is my future mother-in-law, Prugilla," Delphinium announced. "And these ladies are her sisters, and nieces, and cousins and aunts."

The only goblin woman Cory had ever seen before was Natinia Blunk, the attorney who had prosecuted the guilds. These women were mostly older than Natinia, and they all seemed far less fearsome than male goblins, including Officer Deeds, her future stepfather.

"It's very nice to meet you," said Cory. "But I still don't understand how you can kidnap me and think there won't be consequences. What about Blue and Micah and Quince? Don't you think they're going to be worried and go looking for me?"

"We already took care of that," Delphinium told her. "I sent word that you're all right and that you were coming to help me."

"Somehow, I don't think that will make Blue worry any less," Cory said, shaking her head. After all, he knew exactly how Cory felt about her mother.

"Aside from being a member of my wedding party, I do have one other thing I want you to do," Delphinium told her. "I heard that you wrote a song that moved everyone. I want you to write a love song for me. It can be your wedding gift to me and Wilburton."

"Who?" asked Cory. "Oh, right. Officer Deeds. And you want this song for the day after tomorrow? I don't know if I can write one that fast."

"You'll have to," said her mother. "We just hired Zephyr to play it at my wedding reception."

"It's getting late, Delphinium," Prugilla said. "We need to start soon. Why don't you show your daughter to the room she'll be using and give her something to wear? That dress is disgraceful. I don't know why she'd walk around in a badly stained dress."

Cory looked at Prugilla in amazement. The goblin woman had to know that they had kidnapped her from a wedding reception. No wonder Delphinium and Officer Deeds were so right for each other. Cory's mother was going to fit in the goblin family perfectly!

"I can take her there," said the goblin who had brought Cory to the room. When Cory looked at her again, she realized that the goblin was closer to her own age than she'd realized. Her silver hair had made her seem older, but her skin was smooth and unlined, and the tops of her ears stuck straight up, unlike the older goblin women, whose ear tips were limp.

"My name is Scoota," the girl told her as they left the room. "I'm one of Wilburton's cousins."

"Thanks for helping me today," Cory said. "I was certain that a guild had kidnapped me."

"Why would a guild do that?" Scoota asked.

"I won a court case against them and they aren't happy about it," said Cory.

As they walked down the corridor, Cory looked everywhere. As rare as it was to see female goblins, it was even more unusual to be invited into a goblin home. She was furious at her mother for putting her in this position, but Cory wasn't about to pass up the opportunity to see how goblins lived.

"Is this Prugilla's home?" asked Cory.

Scoota laughed. "This isn't anyone's home. This is the female enclave. We use it when we're preparing for weddings. It's set aside specifically for females to hold ceremonies, retreats, and anything else from which the males are excluded. You'll never see any males past that door where they left you. They think we do awful things in here, but we really don't. As long as the males believe it, though, they'll leave us alone. Most males think we're worse than they are."

"Is that why they said, 'Have fun,' and laughed?" asked Cory. "They thought you were going to torture me?"

"Something like that. Once upon a time, goblin females might have, especially an outsider like you, but times have changed and so have we. The males think we still torment the bride's family, but we don't. It's sort of like a big party, except you'll have to take part in some ceremonies. Even those aren't so bad. You'll see."

"Why did they knock me out and leave me in a dark room, then carry me to you in the dark?" Cory asked her.

"The males still want everyone to think they're tough and scary, but they aren't nearly as bad as they pretend they are. Don't get me wrong; they used to be truly horrible, but they had to give up their old ways when we started trying to fit in with the rest of fey society."

"The ogres had to change their ways, too," said Cory.

Scoota nodded. "Just like the ogres, only goblin males still don't want their females to go out in public. Some of us do, though. More every day, actually. Here we are. You'll be using this room until the wedding," Scoota said as she opened a door.

A fairy light went on as soon as they stepped inside. "This is so bright and pretty," Cory said. The room wasn't very big, but the low bed had a floral coverlet in blues and purples, and a braided rug that was different shades of blue. There was a comfortable-looking chair in one corner and a wooden trunk in the other. Ink sticks and a sheaf of leaves lay on a low table by the bed.

Cory crossed over to the table and picked up an ink stick. "Are these for me?" she asked.

"Your mother said you needed them to work on your song. I think it's great that you're in a band. Goblins aren't known for music. We sing sometimes, but it hurts everyone's ears, even our own. Here, change into this," Scoota said, opening the trunk and taking out a simple shift. "It's one size fits all, so it should work just fine until we can get your dress cleaned."

"I don't think you'll be able to get this out," Cory said, touching the stain on her dress.

"You'd be amazed at what goblins can do," Scoota replied. "I'll wait for you in the hall. Come out when you've changed. We don't have much time."

It took Cory only a few minutes to change out of her dress and into the shift. Although it didn't have much shape to it, Cory didn't think it looked too bad. Leaving the bridesmaid's dress on the bed, she joined Scoota in the corridor. "Where are we going now?" she asked.

"Just down the hall. You're going to do something with your mother. When you're finished, I'll see you at dinner."

"What do I have to do?" asked Cory.

"My aunt Prugilla will explain it all," Scoota said. "Here we are. I'll see you in a little while."

The room that Cory entered wasn't very big. Her mother and grandmother were already there, seated in stiff-looking chairs across from each other. When Prugilla saw Cory, the goblin woman pointed to the only other chair and said, "Sit down."

As soon as Cory sat, three older goblin women entered the room and took up positions behind the chairs. Cory noticed that each one held a long pin in her hand.

"Delphinium has been performing this rite for the past few days, so she knows what to expect," said Prugilla.

"It's very simple, really. All you have to do is cry for one hour. According to tradition, this will help the bride use up all her tears so she'll have a happy marriage. Deidre, Cory, you will cry along with her to show your support. If you don't cry, you're dooming Delphinium to a bad marriage and we all know you don't want that. When you've cried for one hour, we'll go have supper. You may start crying now."

"What?" said Cory. "I can't cry just because you tell me to!"

"You have to try, Cory," said Delphinium. "If you don't, they'll make you. Think of something sad—like the time you found that dead squirrel on the road and cried all afternoon."

"I was five!" Cory exclaimed.

"You're not crying yet!" said the goblin woman standing behind her. "You can stop one hour from the time you start."

"Oh, Cory! I wish you'd do what I ask for once! Is it so hard to please your mother?" Delphinium asked as tears began to trickle down her cheeks.

"Well, I'm not crying on command!" Deidre announced. "I'll sit here for an hour, but you won't get a single tear out of . . . Ouch! Did you just poke me with a pin?" She turned around to face the woman behind her, who was poised to jab her again.

"I told you they'd make you cry if you didn't do it on your own!" wailed Delphinium. "Now cry, darn you!"

"Jab me again and you're the one who'll be crying!" Deidre told the goblin woman who had poked her.

"Wait!" Cory said as the woman behind her raised her arm.

The goblin woman jabbed Cory's arm anyway.

Cory yelped and gave her an angry look. "I'm trying to think of something sad."

"You can't think of anything sad because I've given you such a good life," said Delphinium. "You don't have any sad memories."

"You know that isn't true, Mother," Cory told her. "Ow!" The goblin woman had poked her in the shoulder.

"Mother, think about all the young men who didn't come home from the Troll Wars," said Delphinium. "Think about your cousin Andykins. You told me that he was killed the day he reached the front!"

"He was such a nice young man," said Deidre as the first tears sparkled in her eyes. "He always brought me candy when he came to visit."

"I remember how all my friends had birthday parties every year and you got mad when I asked if I could have one!" Cory told her mother. "But that doesn't make me sad. It makes me angry."

The goblin woman jabbed Cory's arm again.

"Ow!" Cory exclaimed. "And you never went to any of my concerts at school because you said they were a waste of your time. That makes me mad, too!"

"I was busy," Delphinium replied.

"You could have made time for me!" Cory half shouted. "But siding with the guilds against me tops everything! You could have stood up for me, Mother!"

"You were wrong to turn against the Tooth Fairy Guild, Cory," said her mother. "I couldn't take your side when you were wrong."

The goblin jabbed her again. "Will you cut that out?" Cory said as tears of frustration welled in her eyes.

"Very good, Cory! Think about how much it hurts. Think about how you're trying and you keep getting jabbed with a pin anyway," said her mother.

And then Cory really began to cry.

"That's it!" shouted Delphinium. "You're crying!"

"What are you thinking about, Cory? It must be really sad," asked Deidre.

"I'm thinking about how I never could make my mother happy, and that I wish I wasn't here," Cory said.

"And it's enough to make you cry!" exclaimed Delphinium. "I must have done something right raising you!"

It wasn't easy to cry for an entire hour, but Cory got better at it after a while. When the hour was up, Prugilla escorted them to a dining room where the other goblin women were already seated and waiting. They congratulated the new arrivals as if they'd done something marvelous, then dug into the dishes as they were placed on the tables.

Cory sat next to Scoota and as far from Delphinium as she could get. After crying for so long, she still felt miserable and not very talkative. She was surprised to see her mother talking and laughing with the goblin women as if she hadn't just been sobbing into a handkerchief. It only reinforced the thought that she'd never understand Delphinium.

Although she tried to answer Scoota's questions, she couldn't make herself eat. Crying had made her lose her appetite, and the fact that most of the dishes had meat in them didn't help. As soon as she could, Cory excused herself from the table and returned to the room where she'd sleep. If she had to write a song, she needed to get started. Anything to make the time pass until she could leave.

Her dress was gone when she stepped into the room, and in its place she found another shapeless shift. After getting ready for bed, she sat on the covers, staring at the ink stick in her hand. At first she was convinced that she didn't have anything to say and could never get a song about love done in time, but she soon found that love was one topic that evoked an outpouring of feelings in her. Cory stayed up half the night working on the song.

CHAPTER
10

Cory woke the next morning feeling much more like her usual self. She ate the cooked grains she was offered at breakfast, politely declining all the meats and eggs. After everyone was finished, Prugilla announced that it was time for the bride to cry again, so Delphinium, Deidre, and Cory trooped down the corridor to the room with three chairs and took their seats. This time Cory was able to cry right away. Thinking about love all night with its attendant hopes and fears, highs and lows, had left her with plenty of ideas that she could use to make her cry.

She was sitting silently with tears streaming down her face when her mother turned to her and said, "I'm glad you decided to help me. The more we cry, the more

Wilburton's family will know how much we want this marriage to work."

Cory smiled through her tears, not feeling the need to tell her mother the real reason she was crying. This time her tears were those of joy. After all, if her mother married a goblin, she would probably be too busy to harass Cory anymore. Yes, she wanted the marriage to work, but not for the same reasons as her mother's.

Although Deidre still had a hard time crying, they finally got through their hour of misery. They were leaving the room when Delphinium turned to Cory and said, "How is the song coming along?"

"Surprisingly well," Cory replied. "I'll need only a few more hours to work on it. It should be ready to rehearse with Zephyr later tonight."

"Oh, you're not going to rehearse with them," said Delphinium. "They aren't allowed in the goblin warren until the day of the wedding."

"Then how are we supposed to play it together? We have to practice to get it right!"

Delphinium shrugged. "I'm sure you'll think of something."

"Come with me, Delphinium, you need to get ready," Prugilla said, taking her by the arm.

Delphinium looked confused. "Ready for what?"

"The next rite, of course," Prugilla replied. "You'll see your mother in just a few minutes, Cory. Scoota will take you where you need to go."

"Do you know what we're doing next?" Cory asked the goblin girl as they started walking.

Scoota nodded. "Yes, and your mother isn't going to like it one bit."

"She won't get hurt, will she? We don't get along, but I won't do anything to hurt her," said Cory.

"Of course not! No one gets hurt in this ceremony! But they do scream a lot," Scoota said with an evil-looking smile.

They walked farther down the corridor than they had before to a room with bare stone floor and walls. Deidre and all the goblin women joined them over the next few minutes. When Delphinium came in wearing a robe and goggles, she looked nervous and very uncomfortable.

Goblin women started walking around the room handing out buckets filled with stinky, black slop. Cory was wondering what she was supposed to do with it, when Prugilla gestured to Delphinium. Wearing a pained look on her face, Delphinium took off the robe so that all she was wearing were the goggles. Cory gasped. She had never seen her mother naked before, and she certainly didn't want to now.

She stood there, trying not to look at her mother, as the goblin women around her reached into their buckets and pulled out handfuls of the black stuff. Prugilla was the first to toss some at Delphinium, who cried out in dismay. After that, goblin women threw the slop randomly, covering Cory's mother until she was dripping with it.

"This is called the Glopping of the Bride," said Scoota. "All the female members of the bride's family, both old and new, have to do it. If you don't, we'll think that you don't want to see our two families joined."

Cory didn't want to do it. Although she didn't like her mother and rarely got along with her, she'd never wished her harm and hated the thought of anyone hurting her. Even so, it looked as if Cory had to throw the glop, whether she wanted to or not. When she looked up, her mother was standing with her back straight and her arms crossed over her chest. Black slop covered the goggles, making it impossible to see through them. At least Cory wouldn't have to look her mother in the eyes when she did this.

Reaching into the bucket, Cory grabbed a fistful and threw it at her mother. She heard a gleeful shout and turned to see her grandmother throwing the muck as fast as she could. Apparently, Deidre had no reservations about "Glopping" the bride.

Cory reluctantly emptied her bucket one glob at a time. When everyone was finished, Delphinium was ushered from the room to loud and joyful cheers. A few goblin women left and came back bearing buckets of clean water, soap, towels, and mops. While some of the women washed the floor, the rest washed the black muck from their hands and arms, then left the room looking very pleased with themselves.

"You'll be involved in one more ceremony after lunch," Scoota told Cory. "But it's a private one. Only you, your mother, and your grandmother will meet with Prugilla and two of her sisters. My mother is one of the sisters."

"It doesn't involve tossing things at people, does it?" asked Cory.

Scoota shook her head and laughed. "No, and no one has to take her clothes off, either."

Cory sat with Scoota again and ate salad for lunch. Her mother, washed and wearing clean clothes, sat with Prugilla. The Glopping ceremony seemed to have endeared her mother to the goblins, and they treated her more warmly than they had before. Deidre was also in a good mood, talking and laughing with the goblins seated around her. Neither her mother nor her grandmother seemed to dread the next ceremony the way Cory did.

The third and final ceremony took place in the room with all the couches. When Cory heard what it was, she wasn't sure it should even be called a ceremony. "These are two of my sisters, Grunnel and Peaches. They'll be helping me with our Goblin Marriage Counseling," Prugilla said as they all sat down. "We do this regardless of who is getting married. However, we feel it's even more important when a goblin is marrying a non-goblin."

"Do very many goblins marry non-goblins?" asked Cory.

"This is the first in our family," Prugilla told her. "We couldn't believe it when he told us, but considering how handsome and charismatic Wilburton is, we shouldn't have been surprised. He was out of the warren working with non-goblins and was bound to catch some lady's eye."

Cory laughed, then covered it with a cough when she realized that Officer Deeds's mother wasn't joking. Deidre looked as if she'd tasted something really terrible. Cory hoped her grandmother wasn't about to say what she was really thinking.

"You know I was married once before," said Delphinium. "How is being married to a goblin any different?"

"Goblin men are very strong-willed," said Prugilla. "They expect to have every little thing their way and can be very nasty if it isn't. I've been married for sixty-seven years, and my husband still thinks he's in charge. That's because I know how to handle him. For instance, when you want something, suggest it in a way that will make him think he thought of it himself. Then continue to let him think it was his idea, even when it grates on your nerves every time he crows about his own brilliance."

"Really?" said Grunnel. "I always let my husband think he's right, until he isn't. Then I set him straight, even if it means kicking him out of the cave."

"I've never kicked my husband out of the cave," declared Peaches.

"That's because when you get in a big fight with him, you come running to my cave," said Grunnel.

"Or mine," Prugilla added.

"I don't come to your caves because we're fighting!" said Peaches. "I come over because he snores so loudly I can't get any sleep! We fight as much as any other happily married goblins. Why else do you think we've stayed together as long as we have? I always say, 'Never go to bed angry. Stay up and fight it out!'"

"When I said that goblin husbands can be nasty if they don't get what they want, just keep in mind that the only way to win a fight with a goblin is to be nastier than he is," Prugilla told Delphinium. "I've lived by that rule every day of my married life and we're both very happy. Goblin husbands expect nastiness. They don't really understand anything else."

"Do you have any suggestions that don't have to do with fighting?" asked Delphinium.

"Of course!" said Grunnel. "You should always tell your husband what you want. He's probably too thick-headed to figure it out for himself."

Peaches shook her head. "I believe in being subtle. If my husband forgets to buy me a gift for an important event, like my birthday or our anniversary or any of the fifty-three goblin holidays, I make lists of gifts I'd like and leave them on his pillow, or next to the toilet, or on his dinner plate. If he's too thick-headed to get the hint, I tape the list to his forehead when he's sleeping. Once, I even used an ink stick to write it on his belly."

"Fifty-three goblin holidays!" cried Cory. "Do you really celebrate them all?"

"I do if it means I get presents," Peaches told her.

"Well, I think we can all agree that communication is very important in a marriage," said Prugilla. "If your husband does something you don't like, tell your mother-in-law about it. She'll make him change his ways. And since I'm going to be your mother-in-law, Delphinium, know that you can count on me!"

❯❯➤

When Cory learned that she wasn't needed for any other marriage preparations that day, she returned to the room she'd slept in to work on the song. Both the music and the lyrics had been in the back of her mind ever since she got up that morning, and she couldn't wait to get her new ideas down on leaf. It was a good song—she could feel it. It might even be her best so far. But then, it was a topic that she knew a lot about, without ever consciously learning it.

Cory got busy right away. She had a lot to do before morning. Not only did she have to finish the song, but she'd have to make copies for all the members of Zephyr. It would have been a lot easier if they could have rehearsed her new song at least once!

CHAPTER
_11_

Although the goblins had returned Cory's bridesmaid's dress without even the hint of a stain, goblin
tradition demanded that she wear another shapeless
sheath with a pair of short pants underneath, this time
in lime green. Apparently, the goblins had decided that
was the color of the Fleuren household, because Deidre
was wearing the same color.

No one had told Cory where the wedding was going
to be held, but she assumed it would be in another cave
in the warren. She was surprised when they paraded
down the length of the corridor to a door that opened
onto a lovely forest glade. They didn't have to walk far
before they came to a large clearing that was already
filled with goblins.

"Prugilla invited two hundred and seventeen goblins," Scoota told her. "Your mother invited her friends from the Tooth Fairy Guild, plus her family."

"That's a lot of goblins," Cory said as she looked around the clearing. When she was younger, she'd been terrified of goblins. But after getting to know Natinia Blunk and Officer Deeds, she'd learned that goblins were people, too. Even so, seeing so many in one place was a little disconcerting. It also felt odd to be one of the tallest people there. Very few goblins stood over five feet tall.

"Actually, this is considered to be a small wedding," said Scoota. "We're using one of the minor clearings for it. We hold all our weddings outside. It's a lot easier to clean up afterward. Now, you and your grandmother have to come with me. You'll see your mother again in a little while."

Cory and Deidre followed Scoota through the crowd of goblins to the middle of the clearing. Quince was already there and she shouted when she saw Cory. "We thought something awful had happened to you!" Quince cried as she came running and threw her arms around Cory. "We looked everywhere! I thought Blue was going to go on a rampage, until we got the message from your mother saying that you were all right. Even then I was afraid he was going to do something drastic."

"It was awful at first," Cory told her. "But then I met Scoota and she explained everything to me. Is Blue here?"

Quince nodded. "He's with Micah and your grandfather. They're on the other side of this circle. Do you have any idea what we're supposed to do next?"

"None at all," Cory said, seeing an older female goblin approaching. "But I think they're about to tell us."

The goblin stopped and pointed to Deidre. "You, stand here," she said. "Now all of you ladies get behind her."

At first Cory thought that the goblin meant just her and Quince, but when she turned around she saw that Scoota and all the other female goblins who had been in the enclave with them were also getting in line.

"Good," said the older goblin as she walked to the side. "Now face this way and lie down on your stomachs."

"What?" Quince squeaked. "I'm wearing my best dress. I'm not lying on the ground in this!"

Scoota and all the other goblins were already starting to lie down. Even Deidre was on her knees and about to stretch out. "I think you have to," Cory whispered to Quince. "It must be part of the ceremony."

"I'd better not get grass stains on this dress!" Quince said as she lay down beside Cory.

"If you do, I'm sure the goblins can get them out!" Cory told her.

"This is so weird!" said Quince.

Cory laughed. "This is nothing compared to what my grandmother and I have been through!"

"Quiet, you two!" ordered Deidre. "I want to hear what they're saying."

"I'm explaining this for the sake of the newcomers," announced an old male goblin. "I know everyone else is familiar with what comes next."

A ripple of laughter ran through the crowd and more than one goblin nodded.

"All right, groom on bride's side, bride on groom's side," the old goblin continued. "Let's get this wedding started!"

Scoota and the other female goblins shifted around as if to get more comfortable. When Cory raised her head and peeked over her grandmother, she saw Wilburton Deeds walking toward them wearing loose pants, a shapeless shirt in bright yellow, and nothing on his big, lumpy feet that were two different sizes. She was sure he was going to stop when he reached Deidre, but he kept walking, stepping on Cory's grandmother. Deidre went "Ooof!" but didn't say anything, then he was stepping on Cory. She grimaced as his foot pressed her into the grass, then he was onto Quince, who gasped. No one moved until he had reached the end of the line. When the old goblin clapped once, they all stood up and brushed themselves off.

"What the heck was that?" Quince whispered to Cory.

"Just the beginning, I'm afraid," Cory whispered back.

"It's supposed to show that the couple has the support of both families," Scoota told them.

Wilburton was walking behind the females to the front of the line when a group of male goblins tackled him. Although he struggled against them, Cory didn't think he was trying too hard, and actually saw him laughing. While some goblins held him down, others tied his legs together with a rope. One of the goblins had brought a sack that he held open for the others. Each of the goblins reached in and pulled out a fish. Gathering around the groom, they began to beat the soles of his feet with the fish and didn't stop until the fish were falling apart in their hands. When the goblins finally untied him and let him up, Wilburton's legs were covered with fish blood and scales.

"I'm glad they didn't do that before he walked on us," Quince whispered to Cory.

"Now comes the fun part," Scoota said as the female goblins in their group started walking toward the center of the circle.

Cory and Quince joined them just as Delphinium showed up wearing a bright yellow shift and holding a huge bouquet of flowers. The old male goblin stood next to her while the females formed a circle around them. "Now what?" Cory asked Scoota.

"This is the Bridesmaid's Blockade," Scoota told her. "We have to keep Wilburton from reaching Delphinium."

"How do we do that?" asked Quince.

"However you can," said Scoota. "I have a good left hook, but my mother prefers kicking."

Stunned, Cory turned to look at her. "We're supposed to fight him?"

"You will if you want to stop him," said Scoota. "He's going to try to drown Delphinium next."

"What?" cried Cory. "Then he's not getting near my mother!"

"That's the spirit!" crowed Scoota. "Watch out! He's looking for a weak spot in the circle and he's coming this way."

Cory turned toward Wilburton. He was walking around the circle, eyeing the line of females as if appraising their possible strengths and weaknesses. The females backed up until they were shoulder to shoulder, leaving no space in between.

Cory braced herself. She'd never physically fought anyone before, and had no idea what to do, but she wasn't going to let Wilburton get anywhere near her mother.

When she glanced at Quince, her friend was holding her hands stiffly in front of her.

"I've got this," said Quince. "I took self-defense classes last year. There's no way he's getting past me!"

Wilburton stopped in front of Cory and Quince, and grinned. "Perfect!" he said, and lunged at them. Quince whacked him across the nose, which seemed to surprise him. He was raising his arms to block her when Cory kicked him in the shins and Deidre clapped his ears with both hands. As he staggered to the left, Scoota punched him in the jaw. And then the female goblins next to her pounced on him, pummeling him until he backed away.

"You can do it!" a goblin male in the crowd shouted.

All the males started shouting encouragement to Wilburton as he circled the females. Cory didn't see what he did next, but she could tell from the shouting and the way the circle moved that he was attacking again. The females beat him back three times. The next time he attacked he was close enough that Cory could see him. When one goblin tried to punch him, he moved under her blow and kicked her legs out from under her. She fell, taking down the two females next to her.

In an instant, Wilburton jumped over her and ran to Delphinium. Scooping her up, he held her high and shouted in triumph, "She's mine!"

The male goblins roared, which Cory thought was a truly frightening sound. She expected them to do something, but instead the old goblin began to talk to Delphinium and Wilburton in words that Cory couldn't quite make out.

"What's he saying?" she asked Scoota.

"He's speaking in ancient Goblinese. It's something about how the next thing they do will be a real test of their love. He just wished them both good luck. And there they go! Wilburton is going to try to drown her."

"That's for real?" asked Quince. "I thought you said that just to make us fight him."

"No, it's for real, all right," said Scoota. "See! He's carrying her to the lake."

The big circle of goblins opened up to let Wilburton through. As he ran past, they all started to follow him, but not one of them tried to stop him.

"We can't let him do this!" Cory cried. "Why isn't anyone doing anything?"

Scoota shrugged. "It's part of the ceremony. If he truly loves her, she'll be fine."

"I need to get there. I need to stop him!" Cory cried, trying to push her way through the crowd.

Scoota grabbed her from behind. "Don't, Cory. He's not going to hurt your mother. I've seen how much he loves her. This just proves it to everyone else. You have to let them do this if the goblins are ever going to consider them truly married."

"Your mother had to know what she was getting into when she agreed to a traditional goblin wedding, Cory," said Quince. "She's not the type of person to go into this blindly."

Cory nodded. "You're right about that," she replied. "But I still want to make sure she's all right."

"Then let's go," Scoota said, and took Quince and Cory by the hands. Crying, "Make way!" so that the crowd parted to let them pass, she ran with them through the goblins, and past the trees surrounding the lake.

When they finally caught sight of the bride and groom, Wilburton was tying rocks to Delphinium's legs. Cory gasped when she saw what he was doing.

"He's really serious about this," said Quince.

"He has to be," Scoota told her. "It's part of the ceremony."

Cory didn't care about the ceremony or what a bunch of goblins thought about her mother's marriage. She wasn't going to let this happen. Letting go of Scoota's hand, she dashed to the water's edge, but by then Wilburton had already set Delphinium in a small boat and was rowing her into the lake.

Cory could swim, but not very well. Certainly not well enough to catch up with Wilburton, who was rowing with long, powerful strokes. As Cory paced up and down along the shore, the rest of the wedding guests arrived and gathered to watch what happened next. Deidre, Quince, and Scoota had just come to stand beside Cory when Wilburton set down the oars, picked up Delphinium, and kissed her. Then with one fluid motion, he tossed her into the lake.

"No!" Cory cried as her mother sank into the water, the rocks tied to her legs dragging her down.

"He has to rescue her now," Scoota told her. "When they come up, if she's still alive, they're good and truly married."

"Then why isn't he going in after her?" wailed Cory.

"He has to count to make sure she's had time to reach the bottom. This is a very deep lake. Ah, there he goes. He'll have her back up before you know it."

Cory was too worried to stand still. She started pacing back and forth, anxiously watching the water. Blue was standing next to Quince and Scoota when she returned to where they were standing. She ran into his arms when she saw him, then they both watched the water together.

Suddenly, with a whoosh and a shower of water, bride and groom popped to the surface. Even while Wilburton was dragging Delphinium to the boat, Cory could see that her mother was trying to swim on her own.

"She's all right!" Cory told Blue as tears of relief glistened in her eyes.

A cheer went up from everyone on the shore. "Like I said," Scoota shouted at Cory. "She's alive, so they're now well and truly married!"

Blue pulled Cory closer and kissed her. "Congratulations!" he said. "You have a new stepfather."

Cory laughed and said, "Yes, I suppose I do."

"We have to do one last thing before we celebrate," Scoota said. "It's time for the wife-carrying competition. Wife or girlfriend, I should say. It's an obstacle course and this one is supposed to be the best one ever. My boyfriend helped design it. I'll see you later. I have to go find him."

"And I'm going to look for Micah," said Quince as she turned and walked off.

"Finally, we get to do something together," Blue declared. "Where do you suppose this thing starts?"

"Follow the crowd," said Cory. "I'm sure they know where to go."

"When you disappeared from Quince and Micah's wedding reception like that, I was really worried about you," Blue said as they walked. "I was going a little crazy when that note came from your mother. I was sure one of the guilds had done something to you."

"I thought a guild was behind it, too, up until I met Scoota," said Cory. "She's the goblin girl who told us about the wife-carrying competition. She's actually very nice."

"I want to hear all about everything," Blue told her.

"You will," said Cory. "But first we have an obstacle course to conquer and a whole lot of celebrating to do!"

CHAPTER
12

The goblins had set up the beginning of the obstacle course partway around the lake. Cory thought it was complete chaos as husbands found their wives and boyfriends found their girlfriends, but it really didn't take very long before everyone was ready. Only the children and the elderly were allowed to sit this out, so Cory wondered how some of the smaller males were going to carry the larger females.

The bride and groom were in the front. When Wilburton hiked Delphinium onto his back, the other goblins grabbed their partners, too. Cory realized just how strong goblins were when she saw how easily even the smallest adult males picked up the females. Some carried their partners on their backs, while others slung them over their shoulders as if they were sacks of fertilizer.

Blue squatted down so Cory could climb onto his back. She wrapped her arms around his neck and kissed him as he grabbed her legs and stood up. Cory was grateful that the goblins had given her short pants to wear under the dress.

"There are three rules!" shouted the old male goblin. "One, no part of the female must touch the ground from the time you start running to the end of the race. If she does touch the ground, you are disqualified. Rule two, follow the orange markings on the ground to each obstacle. You may not skip an obstacle. There will be spotters along the route to make sure you take on each one. And the third and final rule, there are no other rules! Anything goes! May the best goblin win!"

Although Wilburton started out in the lead, other goblins soon passed him. Blue and Cory were near the back of the pack, so it took them a while to reach the first obstacle. Cory thought the ten-foot-tall, thirty-foot-wide log wall looked daunting, but the goblins swarmed up and over it with the females clinging to their necks. For some reason, she could hear a lot of shouting from the other side.

"Hold on tight!" Blue said when he was close enough.

Cory wrapped her legs around Blue and held her breath as he ran at the wall and jumped, catching the top with his fingers. He pulled them to the top, and was about to drop to the ground on the other side when they both spotted the enormous patch of pricker bushes planted at the bottom. Cory saw at least a dozen goblin couples caught in the bushes, struggling to get out.

Two goblin couples reached the top right after Blue and Cory. The goblin with long, dangling ears and an equally long nose was turning around to climb down the other side, when the goblin next to him reached over and pushed him. The long-eared goblin and his partner fell, shrieking, into the pricker bushes. When the goblin who had pushed him looked at Blue, Cory said, "Don't even think it!" while Blue growled and showed his teeth.

The goblin showed his teeth in a fierce grimace, too, but he backed away before climbing down the wall.

"Ready?" Blue asked Cory.

"Go for it," Cory replied.

Holding on to the top while he positioned himself, Blue let go as he pushed off from the wall with his legs, flinging them past the bushes and the goblins. He landed on his feet with his knees bent, then stood and glanced back at Cory.

"Are you all right?" he asked as she readjusted herself on his back.

"Never better," she said. "What's next?"

Blue started running again, following the goblins in front of him. They were jogging through a forest when he had to stop suddenly. The goblins who had made the course had woven vines between the trees ahead. A mass of goblins were crawling through, trying to find big enough openings.

"If it's not big enough for goblins to get through, what are we going to do?" Cory asked Blue.

"I'm trying to figure that out," Blue replied, eyeing the vines. He studied them for a few minutes, letting some goblins pass him.

Cory was watching three goblins back out of the woven vines to try other approaches when Blue said, "I've got it. Hold on!"

In four strides, he reached the vines. Grabbing hold with both hands, he pulled himself and Cory up the front of the intricate weave, then climbed hand over hand to the top. "Let's see if this is as sturdy as it looks," he said, and started to step up and down, side to side as he crossed the gap from one tied vine to the next.

Although the vines shook beneath their combined weight, Blue soon reached the other side. He was climbing down when the goblins who had been watching him started to follow his example. Before he'd even touched the ground, goblins were swarming past him.

"You are so clever!" Cory said as he held her legs and hiked her higher onto his back.

"Hey, we didn't avoid the obstacle and you didn't touch the ground. It's all good!" Blue said as he started walking.

They were enjoying the shade of the forest when they saw an opening up ahead. A crowd of goblins were arguing on the path. As Blue and Cory drew nearer, they discovered that they had reached a deep gorge that was far too wide to jump. Long vines dangled from tree branches growing out over the ravine, and the goblins were using them to swing across.

The goblins weren't taking turns. Pushing and shoving, they fought to get to the vines first. If they got too close to the edge, other goblins pushed them over. The couples fell, screaming. Perched on Blue's back, Cory could see into the ravine. She was relieved that none of the goblins had been badly hurt and were scurrying around, trying to find a way out.

When one foolish goblin tried to push Blue, the half-ogre growled and pushed him back. The goblin flew a dozen feet and landed on his back, squashing his partner. All the air was knocked out of the female goblin.

When she could catch her breath, she screamed at the male until he stood up again.

A spotter had been watching everything. Stomping over, he pointed at the female and said, "She touched the ground! You two are out!"

The female slapped her partner and jumped off his back. No one but Cory watched as they ambled down the path, holding hands. When she turned around, she saw a goblin fight his way to the front and grab a vine. Kicking another goblin in the face to push himself off, he swung over the ravine and landed on the other side. Instead of letting go of the vine right away, however, he held it while his partner rubbed something on it. When he finally let go, Cory thought the vine looked shiny. By the time the vine swung back, Blue was positioned to grab it.

"Not that one!" Cory cried. "That goblin just put something on it."

Blue stepped back. Another goblin grabbed the vine and jumped, but it slipped through his hands, and he and his partner fell, shrieking.

"That other goblin must have greased it," said Blue. He looked around for a moment while the goblins fought to grab the very same, slippery vine. Finally, he grunted and started walking toward a tree set a little apart from the others. Although the orange markings led all the way to the tree, they were scuffed and partially obscured with leaves.

"You're very observant," Cory told him.

"I'm training to be a FLEA officer," said Blue. "I have to be observant."

Cory glanced back. A number of goblins were watching to see what Blue would do. When he grabbed the vine hanging from the tree, they started to run over.

"I just hope this vine is strong enough to hold us," Blue said, and jumped.

Cory thought the rush of air was exhilarating, then they were on the ground again and letting the vine swing back to the other side.

"That was easy," Blue said.

"I know you're doing all the hard work, but I don't know how much longer I can hold on," Cory told him as he walked.

Blue slipped his arms under her knees and boosted her up. "Put your weight on my arms," he said. "I can hold you like this until we reach the next obstacle."

"Thank you," Cory told him, and sagged with relief.

Although there were still plenty of goblins with them on the course, Cory didn't think there were as many as before. Even now she saw some who had dropped out and were sitting on the side of the path. Occasionally she saw spotters pulling couples off the course when the female touched the ground. However, she had yet to see Micah and Quince, or Delphinium and Wilburton at any of the obstacles. She doubted very much that her grandparents were even taking part.

"This next one should be interesting," Blue said as they reached another group of goblins.

Cory glanced at the ground. The orange markings led straight to a big, hollow log lying on its side. Goblins were going in one couple at a time, with spotters squatting beside the log to watch their progress inside. Some of the goblins waiting to go in were pushing the log back and forth, making it roll so that the goblins inside would fall over. Cory counted four couples removed from the course on the other end of the log.

"You obviously can't ride on my back," Blue said. "So you'll have to ride on my front."

"What do you mean?" asked Cory.

"I'm going to have a tough time fitting in that log as it is. With you on my back, we'd never make it. But if you're under me hanging on, we might stand a chance."

"I'm okay with it if you are," Cory told him.

"Then keep holding on with your arms. Tuck your feet up and I'm going to swing you around so you're facing me. Ready?"

"Ready!" said Cory.

Most of the goblins waiting to reach the log were watching them. When Blue pulled Cory around in front of him, she wrapped her legs around his waist. A few of the goblins tried it as well, dropping their mates in the attempt.

Blue strode to the log, pushing aside the goblins who tried to block his way. When he got down on his hands and knees and started to crawl, Cory tucked her face into his shoulder.

It was dark inside the log except for the light coming from the other end. While Cory concentrated on holding on, she heard Blue grunt every time he scraped his back on the log or looked up and hit his head. She could also hear goblins shouting as they tried to roll the log, but weren't able to with Blue's weight inside. Although Cory was certain she was going to touch the ground when Blue had to crouch lower to get out, she didn't, and the spotter gave them a thumbs-up when they finally emerged from the log.

"How are you doing?" Cory asked, their faces so close that their noses were touching.

"I'm fine," he said. "Although I think I picked up some ants in there."

"You did!" said Cory, brushing one off his chin.

Blue carried Cory in his arms then because neither one was in a hurry to switch back. She knew they'd have to, however, when she saw what lay ahead. The trees ended just a little farther on, and the ground looked wet and marshy. Although the path ended, the orange markings led straight to a series of bare poles set a yard apart. Goblins were holding on to the poles, trying to get from one to the next. Only a few were able to get past the first pole, and the rest fell off at the second. Apparently, the ground below the poles wasn't solid. It was quicksand and the spotters had to pull out the ones who had fallen.

"Do you think you can do this?" Cory asked Blue. "It looks as if it would be nearly impossible even if you weren't carrying me."

"I used to go rock climbing with Macks," Blue told her. "I think I can handle this, but I'm going to need my hands. Keep your arms around my neck and I'll shift you behind me."

"My arms are either going to be very strong after this, or limp noodles," Cory said as he moved her onto his back.

"I'll love you either way!" Blue said with a laugh.

When most of the goblins there had attempted the obstacle and were resting before they tried again, Blue walked up to take his turn. The goblin who had gone before him wasn't able to move on to the second pole, but he was also reluctant to get off. He refused to get down even when other goblins started throwing globs of mud at him. When the spotter finally told him that he had to get down, the goblin slipped off and stomped away, arguing with the female on his back.

After shifting Cory to a more comfortable position, Blue grabbed hold of the first pole and swung himself up. Using his arms to propel him and his legs to grab the next pole, he swung from one to another, almost making it look easy. When he reached the last pole, he jumped down, landing just past the edge of the quicksand.

A lot of the goblins who had been watching Blue seemed to think they could do what he had done. Blue was walking away when the first one fell. Before they were out of sight, the spotters had to haul another three out of the quicksand.

"How many more obstacles are there?" said Cory. "I don't know about you, but I'm hungry!"

"I know," Blue told her. "I can hear your stomach rumbling. There's the next obstacle up ahead. It's a river and I think we have to cross some rapids. I won't need my hands for this. Rest your weight on my arms again."

"Thank you so much!" Cory said as he tucked his arms under her knees. "Thank you for being so sweet and strong and smart and wonderful!"

"Thank you for not weighing much at all!" Blue replied. "It makes it so easy!"

The crowd of goblins had dwindled to a small fraction of the number that had started. With no goblins blocking her view, Cory could see the rows of rocks that led from one side of the river to the other, but the rocks were wet and slippery, and the few goblins who were there were taking their time crossing. Because the rocks were so far apart, the goblins had to jump from one to the next. Intent on getting themselves across, none of them were doing anything to stop the others.

"Here goes!" Blue said, picking an unoccupied row.

His first step was tentative, but his stride was long enough that he didn't need to jump. Moving slowly, he nearly fell once when his foot slipped and he didn't quite have his balance, but he caught himself and made it across.

Cory crowed with delight as he stepped onto the riverbank. "I think I can see the finish line! We're almost there!"

"And I can actually smell food cooking," said Blue. "Look out lunch, here we come! There's just one more obstacle. It's over there in those trees."

"I know you can rock climb, but how good are you with trees?" Cory asked as they drew closer.

There was a path again and the orange markings led to a tall tree right beside it. A rope that must have been at least fifty feet long connected the tree to another farther down the path.

"I've climbed plenty of trees," said Blue. "Although it's been a while."

"This means you have to use your arms again," Cory remarked. "I don't want to complain, but my arms are getting really, really tired."

"We're almost there, darlin'," Blue told her. "Hold on just a little while longer."

A crowd had gathered by the finish line to watch as Blue started climbing the tree. It was a tall tree, but it had good sturdy branches and he was able to climb it without any problems. However, the rope wasn't nearly as thick as the vines that the goblins had used earlier.

"I'm not sure about this," said Blue. "This may not hold us."

"Do you want to quit now?" Cory asked him.

"After all we've done? There's no way I'm quitting now," said Blue. "Hold on, this may be our wildest ride yet!"

Cory hardly breathed as Blue started across the rope, pulling himself forward hand over hand. She looked down only once. Although they weren't nearly as high as they'd been when crossing the ravine, she hadn't been as afraid then as she was now. She had seen what Blue meant about the rope. It might have been sturdy enough for goblins, but she would never have chosen it to support a human-size person, let alone a half-ogre.

They were more than halfway across and Cory was just beginning to think that they might make it all the way when the rope suddenly snapped. Blue held on tightly to the end in his hand as they swung toward the other tree, hitting a branch and bouncing off another until they slammed into the trunk. The tree shivered and leaves fell around them, but Blue didn't let go.

"Blue, you have to let go now!" Cory told him. "Step onto that branch and grab hold of that other one. The ground is right there!"

"Huh?" Blue said, dazed. "Oh, right. Sorry."

Placing his feet securely on the bottom branch, Blue got his balance and looked down. His knuckles were white when he finally opened his hand. "We're almost there, Cory," he said, and shinnied down the tree.

A loud cheer went up from the crowd, and they gathered around as Blue and Cory approached the finish line.

"You can get down now, miss," a goblin shouted.

"Did you hear that, Cory?" asked Blue. "You can get down off my back."

He stopped and waited, but Cory wasn't ready. "Not yet," she said. "I'm not touching the ground until we've crossed the finish line! Telling me to get down might be another goblin trick. Look, there are some goblins coming up behind us. Hurry and get across the line."

"Why should we hurry?" he asked. "The rope broke, so they can't do that obstacle."

"Exactly!" said Cory. "They can come straight here!"

"Oh, right!" Blue said, and broke into a run.

Goblins are fast, but a half-ogre with his girlfriend on his back can still be even faster. Blue crossed the finish line before the goblins, which made them stomp their feet and howl. Cory slid off Blue's back and groaned from the ache in her arms. She was rubbing them when her mother and new stepfather walked up wearing first-place ribbons.

"You won?" said Cory. "How is that possible? We never saw you on the course after the first few minutes. When did you get here?"

Delphinium shrugged. "This was our wedding. Apparently, the bride and groom always win. We started, but we quit when someone reminded Wilburton that we didn't have to run the course."

"We came in second!" Deidre announced as she joined them. She held up her red ribbon and laughed.

"How long have you been here?" Cory asked her as Clayton walked up.

"A few hours, I think," her grandfather said.

"How is that possible?" asked Blue. "We didn't see you on the course either."

"Should we show them, dear?" Deidre asked her husband.

When he nodded, they both turned tiny and Deidre flew into Clayton's arms.

"We flew the course," Clayton said after turning back. "It took us only a few minutes to go through every obstacle. It was actually a lot of fun!"

"You mean you cheated!" said Cory.

"Not at all!" her grandmother replied. "We followed every one of the goblin rules!"

"You and Blue came in third," Delphinium said, handing them each a yellow ribbon. "You also won the consolation prize. It seems they got more fish than they needed to hit Wilburton's feet, so there are plenty left over."

"Our prize is a sack of fish that has probably been left out in the sun all day? Thanks, but no thanks," Cory told her.

"Then you and I will keep them, dearest," Wilburton told his wife. "Rotting fish can be delicious if we cook them just right."

"I think I'll pass on that one," Delphinium said, making a face.

A gong sounded and a goblin shouted, "Food!"

Suddenly, all the goblins who had been waiting with the bride and groom started running to some tables set up just down the path. As Cory and Blue followed, she saw that they had gone nearly full circle and were back by the lake where they had started. Big tables had been set up around the edge of the lake, and each table had one sort of food. A huge table held meat dishes, from roasts to sausages to platters of grilled meat patties. Another table was laid with fish, and a third with fowl. An enormous cake rested in the center of a dessert table, with all sorts of pastries around it. Cory almost laughed when she saw that a tiny table held three small bowls of vegetables.

"We told them we needed some vegetables for the bride's family," said Delphinium. "I suppose we should have been more specific when we talked to the caterers."

"You had this catered?" Cory asked her mother. "We've never hired a caterer before."

"My bride is worth it!" Wilburton said, and kissed Delphinium on the lips.

When they didn't stop kissing, Cory looked away. "Look!" she said, spotting the members of Zephyr. "The band is here."

Grabbing Blue's hand, Cory started walking. "I suppose I'll get used to seeing them kiss, but I can't stomach it yet."

They were working their way through the crowd when Cory almost ran into a young human-looking woman with her hair in six or seven braids who was carrying another platter of meat. "Excuse me," said the young woman. When she looked at Cory, her eyes grew wide and she grinned.

"That must have been a fan," Blue said as he and Cory continued walking.

"That must have been a caterer," said Cory.

"There's our girl!" Olot said when he saw her. "We heard that you'd been abducted. Blue and I were getting a search party organized when he got a note from your mother."

"Oh, Cory! Are you okay? Everyone was so worried!" Daisy said, and gave her a big hug.

"Is everything all right?" asked Chancy. "I know Delphinium said it was, but I've met your mother and I know what she's like."

"Everything is fine," said Cory. "Except Mother made me write a new song and wants us to play it today."

Olot nodded. "We heard all about it. A girl goblin named Scoota gave us the copies you'd made and we've already practiced it a couple of times. It has quite an impact, so we thought we'd play it at the end."

"What do you mean by impact?" asked Blue.

"You'll see," Olot said with a grin.

"I need to warm up," Cory told Blue. "Would you mind getting me something to eat?"

"Sure. I'm looking forward to trying some myself. Goblins love meat as much as ogres do. It's one of the few things we have in common. When you finish your warm-up, I'll be sitting right over there," Blue said, pointing just past the stage where her drums were waiting.

Although the other band members had already practiced, they started warming up with Cory. When she felt she was ready, she grabbed a quick bite from the food Blue had brought, then returned to her drums.

The goblins gathered around the stage, talking and eating, when it looked as if the band was about to begin. When no one introduced Zephyr, Olot shrugged, and they started the concert anyway. They played the songs that the bride and groom had chosen, starting with "Owl Goes A-Hunting." After that they played "Storm-Chased Maid," "Shooting Stars," and "Dusk in the Meadow."

The goblins really seemed to enjoy the nature-based songs, dancing at times and hooting and cheering when each one was over. Cory wasn't sure how they'd react to the song that she'd titled simply "Love Song," but then, she wasn't sure how goblins would react to anything. When the band started to play it, the entire clearing went quiet. After the first few bars, the goblins stood with their heads tilted as if that might help them hear it. Because Cory had yet to play the song on her drums, she started out hesitant at first, but the song built on itself, and her drumming became stronger and more confident. As she sang the lyrics along with her bandmates, the words seemed to gain a strength of their own.

Cory was so caught up in her music that she didn't notice when the goblins began to sway with their eyes glazed over and their mouths partly open. No one moved when it finally ended, but Cory could have sworn she heard a hum of power that quickly faded away. A few heartbeats later, every goblin with a partner turned to his or her loved one and embraced. Blue jumped onto the stage to hug Cory, Olot plucked Chancy from the audience, Skippy hugged his two girlfriends, and Daisy grabbed hold of Perky and kissed him. The song touched even those who didn't have a partner. Tears coursed down Cheeble's cheeks as he smiled.

Delphinium and Wilburton were standing near the stage, holding each other, when Cory's mother turned to her and said, "That was so beautiful! Perhaps I should have gone to your concerts after all."

CHAPTER

13

*F*our days later, Cory was thinking about how nice it was to be home and back to her routine, when Orville knocked on her office door. "Miss Daisy and Miss Marjorie are here to see you," he said. "Would you like me to serve tea on the terrace?"

"That would be lovely, Orville. Thank you," Cory replied as she set down her ink stick. Ever since she got home from her mother's wedding, she had immersed herself in making matches. Visions were coming to her frequently now, and she felt as if she had to make up for the time she'd lost in the goblin warren. Keeping busy also helped her set aside the nastier memories of her visit there. Being kidnapped had been bad enough. Seeing her mother covered in black glop had been even worse.

Although Blue had been very affectionate since their return home, she hadn't seen much of him. When he wasn't at work, he was busy studying for his Culprit Interrogator test, but that didn't mean he wasn't watching out for her. Even though he knew that she had been kidnapped because of her mother's goblin wedding, a once-in-a-lifetime event, he was worried about Cory's security. The day after returning home he had insisted that they hire two more ogres to watch over her. Now no one could get on the property without an ogre interrogation. Visits from angry fairies had stopped completely. Although Cory was happy about that, she wasn't happy that she couldn't step outside without at least one ogre tailing her.

She looked around as she left her office and started down the hallway. Their first day there, the ogres, Cran and Andrue, had tried to follow her around inside the house. She had put an end to that immediately by threatening to terminate their employment. They'd agreed that if they did their job right, no one could sneak into the house anyway, so they took turns patrolling the grounds when Macks wasn't making his rounds with Shimmer.

Cory stepped onto the terrace and found her friends seated at the table. Andrue was already there, standing in the shadows.

"Cory!" Marjorie cried. "How are you? Daisy has been telling me that you've had quite an adventure."

"I guess you could call it that," Cory said, taking a seat at the table. "But my mother is married and that's all that counts now."

"And you have goblin relatives," said Marjorie. "Who would have thought your mother would marry a goblin. Do you know how they met?"

"It was at court, I believe," Cory said. Although she had told Marjorie that she was a Cupid before learning that she shouldn't tell anyone, her friend hadn't believed her. She wasn't about to tell her again.

"We heard something interesting today," Daisy was saying as Orville stepped out the door, carrying a tray. He set down a plate of tiny sandwiches, then poured cups of tea for each of them.

As soon as the putti was gone, Daisy opened her mouth to continue, but Marjorie leaned forward and whispered, "Did you know that someone is standing in the shadows, watching us?" Shielding her hand with her body, she pointed to her left.

"I do know that," Cory whispered back. "That's my bodyguard Andrue. He's an ogre and he's supposed to be there."

"You have a bodyguard?" Daisy said in a regular voice. "I mean, I knew about Macks, but . . . You still have Macks, don't you? He's such a nice guy and I'd hate to think that you fired him just because he broke some furniture at your birthday party."

"I didn't fire Macks," said Cory. "He's still here. In fact, the new guards are friends of his and they all get along very well."

"You have more than one new one?" Daisy said, turning to look around. "Why, are you under attack or something?"

"No," Cory said with a laugh. "I have two new body-guards because Blue is being overprotective. So, what was this interesting thing you heard today?"

"Well," Daisy began, "I met Marjorie for lunch because she's lending me some of the books she's written that are already out of print and she brought them with her. We were sitting in Perfect Pastry when we heard the women at the next table talking. Apparently, there's a young woman calling herself the Little Match Girl who has started making matches. She guarantees that people will fall in love with the person of their choosing. You have to pay her first, then you go to her house, she serves you both a meal, you listen to soft music, and you fall in love. The women were saying that the Little Match Girl has a one hundred percent success rate. Can you believe it?"

"It sounds pretty amazing," said Cory.

"I think she's either a Cupid or a witch with great magical powers," said Marjorie. "That is, if Cupids are really real."

Cory thought that her friend might be giving her a strange look, then decided that she'd imagined it.

"I'm considering taking my new boyfriend to see the Little Match Girl," said Daisy. "His name is Kurt Strong and he has the dreamiest eyes. It's been so long since I felt like I was in love. Maybe it's time for the real thing."

"I wouldn't do that if I were you," Cory told her. "You can't just pick a person and make him love you. Real love doesn't work that way."

Daisy set down her teacup so hard that tea sloshed onto the table. "I didn't come here for you to tell me that it was a dumb idea. You're my friend. You're supposed to be encouraging. You've found the love of your life. Well, I haven't and I'm getting tired of looking. I think it's about time I met my true love, even if I have to make it happen! Come on, Marjorie, coming here was a mistake!"

"I'm sorry, Daisy," Cory said as her friend stood up and grabbed her bag of books. "I thought you wanted my opinion. I'm not going to tell you to do something if I think it's wrong for you."

"Well, you don't have to be so negative!" Daisy said, and flounced off the terrace.

"I'll see you later," Marjorie told Cory. "I'd better go calm her down."

And then Marjorie was gone, hurrying down the steps and around the side of the house.

"That didn't go very well," Cory said as she got to her feet.

Andrue stepped out of the shadows to pull back her chair. "Hey, if anybody would know about love, it's you. You told her the truth, which is what a good friend does."

"Do you know who I am?" Cory asked him.

Andrue nodded. "Macks told me and Cran. He said we needed to know so we would do our jobs right. He said that you're the real deal and we should guard you with our lives. Don't worry. We're not going to tell anyone. Macks knows we're good at keeping secrets."

"I just wish he had talked to me first. I don't know how much of a secret it is if everybody knows," said Cory. "Do you have any idea where he is now? I want to ask him who else he's told."

"He's with the dragon. They were up front on patrol when your friends came. I hope I didn't get Macks in trouble, miss."

Cory sighed. "Not at all. I know he means only the best. Thank you for telling me the truth."

She thought about what she would say to Macks while she walked around the side of the house with

Andrue following ten paces behind. Although she'd prefer not to have Andrue there for her conversation with Macks, she couldn't very well tell him to stop following her. After all, he was just doing his job.

When Cory reached the front yard, she didn't see Macks anywhere, but she did see Daisy and Marjorie waiting for a pedal-bus. Hoping to prompt a vision, she thought about Daisy and tried to *see* her true love, but no other face appeared.

"Are you okay? The way you're staring into space made me think you were having some sort of seizure."

Cory turned toward the voice and saw Poppy, the fairy who lived next door. "I was just thinking about something," Cory told her. "How are you today?"

"Fine and dandy," Poppy said. She eyed Andrue, who had hung back but was obviously following Cory. "You sure have a lot of ogres hanging around. Can we talk in front of him?"

"Of course," Cory replied. "What did you want to talk about?" She had nothing to say to the girl, but she didn't want to be rude to a neighbor.

"Word is going around that someone calling herself the 'Little Match Girl' is making matches between couples and the matches really work. She does it with one date and they fall in love every time. If I were looking for a match, should I go to her or you?"

"I don't know this person, so I have no idea what her abilities might be, but I'm not taking on clients for money anymore," said Cory. "I really can't help you."

"I can pay you whatever you're asking," Poppy told her.

"Sorry, but it isn't a matter of payment," Cory said.

"Uh-huh," said Poppy. "I get it. You only help your friends. See you around!"

Cory shook her head as Poppy walked off. This was the second time that she had asked Cory about matchmaking. Either the girl had a memory like a sieve or she was up to something.

When Cory went to bed that night, she was feeling uneasy. Macks had seemed hurt when she asked him not to tell anyone else who she was, almost as if she'd accused him of something terrible. She really wanted to help Daisy, but didn't know how without telling her that she was Cupid and that she would help her if she could. And the more she thought about Poppy and her questions, the more she was certain that the girl was planning something unpleasant. For a moment, she almost missed being back in the goblins' warren, where all she'd had to worry about were the goblins' ceremonies and finishing her song.

Shimmer was out patrolling the grounds with Macks, so Cory went to sleep without hearing the sounds of the little dragon grumbling and shifting in her bed on the floor. Only a few hours after falling asleep, Cory woke to the feel of something cold wrapped around her neck. She struck out, but her hands met cold air. When she touched her throat, the coldness was still there. She wasn't aware of what she was doing when her hands began to glow and give off a heat of their own. Suddenly, the cold was gone, and Cory sat up, rubbing her throat.

She looked around the room, trying to see her assailant. Instead, she saw a shifting in the shadows as something came toward her again. Cory reached to turn on the fairy light, but it refused to turn on. "What do you want?" she cried as she fumbled in her nightstand. "Who sent you?"

Something scratched on the door that opened onto her balcony.

"Cory!" wailed the ghost. It drifted closer and was reaching for her again when her hand closed on the squirt gun that Orville had left for her. The ghost was only a few feet away when she squirted lemon juice at him. He shivered as if shaking off a fly, then kept coming.

Cory squirmed out of bed on the opposite side and ran to the balcony door. Something cold brushed the back of her neck as she yanked the door open. "You can't escape me," cried the ghost.

The little dragon ran into the room. "Shimmer, get him!" Cory cried, pointing at the ghost.

Tail lashing, the dragon pounced, passing right through the figure to the other side. The ghost laughed and came after Cory again, but Shimmer spun around, opened her mouth, and flamed.

"Use your inside flame!" Cory shouted.

Although the flame shrank, it was still enough to heat the ghost. Wailing, the ghost fled out the window into the night.

"Miss Cory, are you all right?" Cran hollered as he threw open the door and ran into the room.

Orville, Creampuff, and two other putti were right behind him, holding squirt guns. "I smelled a ghost again!" cried Creampuff. Sniffing, the little chef followed her nose to the balcony door.

"There was a ghost here, but Shimmer chased it away," said Cory. "The squirt gun you gave me didn't work, Orville."

"Maybe the lemon juice needs to be fresh," he said, scratching his bald head. "I did fill that squirt gun last week."

"Whatever the case, I want Shimmer in here with me when I go to sleep," said Cory. "At least until we find out why a ghost keeps visiting me and I can make it stop."

CHAPTER
14

Macks borrowed Lionel's solar car to drive Cory and Laudine to the New Town Semi-Annual Witches' Trade Show the next morning. "The show is 'For Trade Only,' which means that only witches are allowed in," said Laudine. "I can get you in as my guest, Cory, although it is a little unusual."

"Uh, what about me?" asked Macks. "I'm supposed to stay with Cory to protect her. Can't I be your other guest?"

"I'm afraid not, Macks. We're really not supposed to take non-witches to the trade shows. I'm actually pushing the limit by taking in one. I could never get away with taking two."

"Then how will I keep her safe?" Macks asked, looking worried.

"Leave that up to me," said Laudine. "No one will bother her while I'm around. Now, if you'll excuse us, Cory and I have some confidential matters to discuss."

Laudine reached into her purse and took out a small bottle. She uncorked it, revealing a stick with a circle on the end. Holding the circle to her lips, she blew a bubble that continued to grow even after she held it at arm's length. As the bubble got bigger, it engulfed Cory and Laudine, shimmering around them with all the colors of the rainbow. Suddenly, Cory could no longer hear sounds coming from outside the bubble.

"There," said the witch. "Now no one can hear us. I'm not as concerned about Macks as I am about someone who might use a spell to listen in. This will distort the sound and the image. I wanted to tell you that I sent Zarinda Scard a ticket to the show with a note that she should come early today. We'll have to look for her as well as Darkin Flay."

"Thank you, Laudine!" said Cory. "I'm sure I would have found them eventually, but you're making it much easier."

"I'm glad I'm able to help," Laudine replied. "So many people think only of themselves. It's about time people started helping one another, especially when it comes to true love. Now tell me, did something happen at your house last night? I wasn't able to sleep and was getting a cup of warm milk when I saw the lights go on in some upstairs windows."

"It was another ghost, although it might have been the same one. I hate to admit it, but they look and sound the same to me. I have yet to find out what they want or who sent them."

"I bet the faction I told you about is behind it," said Laudine. "They often use ghosts to frighten people. I've heard they even have them on retainer. They're probably after you because someone has seen us together. They're working hard to get me to step down. I wouldn't put it past them to go after my friends."

"Have they sent ghosts to your house, too?" asked Cory.

"Once," Laudine told her. "But I frightened it so badly that they never sent another."

"Some friends stopped by yesterday to tell me about a girl who calls herself the Little Match Girl," said Cory. "Have you heard about her?"

"I have, actually," Laudine replied. "I plan to visit her to see if she's using unlicensed magic."

"Just like you thought I was when I first moved into Grandfather's," Cory said.

Laudine gave her a rueful smile. "I'm afraid so. I'm still sorry I went after you like that."

Cory shrugged. "And I'm sorry that we have to keep it a secret that I'm Cupid. It's making a lot of things difficult. If you wouldn't mind, when you go see the Little Match Girl, I'd like to go with you. Something about her doesn't sound quite right."

"I think everything about her doesn't sound right!" said Laudine. "Of course you can go. Maybe you'll see something that I won't."

Macks tapped on the bubble and pointed. Laudine opened the bottle again and held up the stick. When she held it against the bubble, the shimmering colors disappeared back into the bottle and Cory could hear everything again.

"We're almost there, ladies!" Macks announced from the front seat.

Cory glanced out the window. They were approaching a big, windowless building with a double front door. "I don't know how long we'll be inside, Macks," said Cory. "Did you bring your mazes?"

"I sure did," Macks replied. "I'm working on the last one in the book and I'm making it extra tough."

When Laudine raised an eyebrow, Cory explained, "Macks creates mazes. He's really very talented."

"That's wonderful!" said Laudine. "I've never been very good at solving mazes. Most witches aren't. I suppose it comes from relying on magic to find our way."

Macks pulled up to the front entrance and jumped out to open the solar-car door for them. Witches were thronging to the event, but no one bothered to look at them until Laudine stepped out. Seeing the president of Witches United, the witches who were closest stepped aside to let her pass. A few called out to her, while others waved or nudged their friends and pointed.

Cory felt like she was with a celebrity as she followed Laudine into the building. Although she hadn't given it much thought, now that she was inside she couldn't help but be excited. Rows of stalls filled the building, some no more than one table wide, while others were five or six times bigger. Every stall offered something related to magic. Cory could feel the air around her quivering with magic and power. She reminded herself of a gawking tourist on her first trip to New Town.

"Where should we start?" she asked Laudine.

"If Darkin Flay is selling ingredients for magic, we should start there," said Laudine. "I believe that's usually in the back corner on the right."

"Is this show always this crowded?" Cory asked as they tried to make their way through the milling people. Although Laudine had been recognized outside, there were so many people in the building that it was hard to spot one individual unless you were right next to her.

"I'm afraid so, although the last night is the worst," Laudine told her. "Merchants drop their prices then so they don't have as much to haul away. But you can't count on getting something you really want on the last night because everything is so picked over. Stay close to me. We don't want to get separated."

Cory tried to keep up with Laudine, but people were pushing and shoving in every direction, and there was so much to see that it was easy to get distracted. Even the people themselves were interesting. Although most were dressed in ordinary clothes, some wore outfits that made them stand out. She saw a few people wearing long, flowing capes that glittered when the wearers moved; Cory was impressed until she saw them for sale at one of the stands. There were shirts and dresses that lit up and others that seemed to pull light into them, making everything around them look gray and lifeless. When Cory ran into a group of people walking together who wore long, ancient-looking robes, they spoke to her in a language she couldn't understand before moving on.

"Cory, this way," Laudine said, leading her around a group that had stopped to haggle with a stall owner selling potted plants used in spells and potions.

Cory slowed to read the labels on angelica, dill, garlic, clover, gardenias, heliotrope, fennel, mugwort, nettle, forget-me-nots, and lemon verbena. There were even yew and crab apple saplings for sale. The most interesting plants she saw, though, were labeled "Dead Men's

Fingers," and actually looked like real fingers sticking out of the soil.

When they were finally past the table, they came to some of the bigger stalls where witches and wizards were selling magic carpets. Some of the carpets had floral designs, some designs were abstract, and a few were simply blocks of color. "They're beautiful!" Cory said as they passed the stall labeled "Hocus-Pocus Magic Carpets."

"If you think these are beautiful, wait until you see the next two stalls," said Laudine. "Hocus-Pocus sells low-end carpets. Zippity-Doo-Dah sells the mid-range carpets. See, there they are. I've been reading about their new line that they're calling 'Air to Spare Deluxe.' I think they hope to compete with the high-end carpets that Arabian Dreams sells. One of these days I might look into them. Their ads make them sound very nice."

A wizard stepped out of the stall area, zeroing in on Laudine as if he'd overheard her. "Hello! I see you've noticed our top-of-the-line model. It just came out and is already our bestseller. Come in! Take a seat! You'll never find a more comfortable ride than on our 'Air to Spare Deluxe' model! Confidentially, I used to work for Arabian Dreams and this model is much better than anything they carry. Here you go! This pattern is one of my particular favorites. I have one just like it at home."

Cory watched as the salesman made the carpet rise and glide behind Laudine. The witch was about to protest when the carpet pushed against the back of her legs, forcing her to sit down. She looked startled as the salesman continued to talk about the carpet.

Cory began to look around, admiring the different patterns as she waited for Laudine. She had found one with a mix of colors that she really liked, when another salesman approached. "Would you like to sign up for our raffle? We're giving away a free carpet every day of the show. You might be the lucky winner of today's prize!"

"I really don't think—" Cory began.

"It's free and there's absolutely no obligation on your part. Just fill out your name and address and you'll have a chance to win that beautiful carpet," he said, pointing vaguely in the direction of the Air to Spare Deluxe models.

"All right," Cory said. Thinking that Blue might really enjoy a flying carpet, she wrote down his name and address. After handing the salesman the card, she turned to look for Laudine. Her friend was standing at the side of the stall, talking to another witch.

Cory was smiling as she walked over to join them, but her smile vanished when she heard what the other witch was saying. "You've already been at this too long,

Laudine. We've all noticed that you don't attend to matters like you once did. You should have relinquished the title years ago. Give some new blood with a fresh outlook a chance to lead the group."

"New blood, Hagatha? Don't you mean that I should let you take over? You're my age! I doubt very much that your outlook is any fresher than mine. I'm not stepping aside for you or any of your cronies." Laudine spotted Cory then and sounded almost relieved when she said, "Ah, there you are, Cory. Ready to go?"

"I sure am," Cory replied, and started back to the main aisle.

Hagatha's eyes narrowed when she heard Cory's name. "You aren't Cory Feathering, are you?"

"Yes," Cory said. "Have we ever met?"

"No, but I've been wanting to meet you," Hagatha told her. "You aren't a witch. What are you doing here?"

"She's my guest," said Laudine. "If you have an issue with that, you can take it up at the next meeting."

"Thank you for the suggestion, Laudine," Hagatha said, but she was looking at Cory when she said it.

"Did you buy a magic carpet?" Cory asked her friend as they walked down the aisle.

Laudine laughed. "No, but it was a close call. That salesman wouldn't listen when I said 'no.'"

"He wasn't the only pushy salesman there," Cory said. "I talked to one who made me fill out a raffle ticket."

"Don't count on winning anything," said Laudine. "The chance that you will is very slim."

"Or none," Cory said with a laugh. "I did it only so he'd leave me alone."

They passed stalls selling brooms next. Cory thought the names of the companies selling them were more interesting than the brooms themselves. "Sweep Stakes," "Brooms R Us," and "The Broom Factory" all made sense, but her favorite was the stall marked "Broom Ha-Ha."

"I bought my first magic wand at a trade show like this," Laudine told her as they passed a stall selling wands. "Back then they were good, sensible wands that could handle real magic. Today they sell all sorts of add-ons. Look at that—you can get lights, flashing or constant. You can also make your wand sparkle every time you use it or have sound effects ranging from chimes to booms to pings. From what I hear, the more you add on, the less reliable the wand. Give me a good old-fashioned wand any day."

"I've seen you do magic without a wand. Do you use one very often?" asked Cory.

Laudine shook her head. "Hardly ever anymore, and then mostly because people seem to expect it. A good witch doesn't need a wand, but it takes years of practice to do without one. Ah, here we are," she said, stopping in front of a stall called "Magic Ingredients." "And if I'm not mistaken, that young man is Darkin Flay."

Cory studied the young man talking to some customers. "That's him all right," she said. "Now we just have to find Zarinda Scard."

"Give her a minute," said Laudine. "I put a little spell on the ticket I sent to her so she'd show up at this booth when we did. Why don't you look around? I'll know when she gets here."

"Are you sure you don't mind?" asked Cory. "I can keep watch while you explore."

"I've seen stalls like this a hundred times and they all sell the same kinds of things. Go ahead," Laudine said. "I'll be right here."

The merchandise at the stall was interesting, although not as interesting as some. Cory found boxes filled with sandalwood, bowls filled with different-colored crystals, jars of soot, and little bags of slippery-elm bark, dried rattlesnake, dried skunk, and starfish. She was examining the crystals when Laudine called to her in a soft voice, "I see her."

Cory turned around. A smartly dressed young woman with bouncing black curls was walking toward the stall. It was Zarinda Scard. Darkin Flay was talking to another customer when Cory held out her hands and thought, *Bow!*

Time stood still when the bow appeared in one hand and the quiver in the other. Pulling the first arrow out of the quiver, Cory read the name "Zarinda Zenobia Scard." With her eye on the young woman who had frozen midstep, Cory set the arrow and took aim. The arrow hit with a soft *plunk* and a puff of sparkles.

Turning to Darkin, Cory took out the second arrow. "Darkin Randall Flay" was written on the shaft. When the arrow hit its mark, the puff of sparkles lit up the corner of the stall where the young man was standing.

Cory dropped her hands as the bow and quiver vanished. She watched as Darkin turned toward the aisle and faced Zarinda. The young woman walked another pace, then stopped as if she'd hit a stone wall. When she turned toward Darkin, their eyes met. Seconds later, they were in each other's arms.

"You're fast," Laudine said, coming up behind Cory.

"I am when I have help like that!" Cory told her. "That was so easy, and it was all because of you. Thank you!"

Laudine shrugged. "I'm glad I was able to be part of it. True love!" she said with a sigh. "It doesn't get any better than that."

"Don't look now, but is that Hagatha Smerch watching us from behind the magic wand display stand?" asked Cory.

"I noticed her following us," said Laudine. "I'm sure she saw new love blossom just then. I can't imagine what she made of it. Now tell me, do you want to go home, or do you want to see more of the trade show?"

"I would like to stay a little while longer," Cory replied. "We didn't see anything on the other side."

"Good!" Laudine declared. "There's a candle maker who comes to every show and she always has her stand there. She makes the most wonderful candles that can put you to sleep in minutes. I'm going to buy a half dozen if she still has that many. She always sells out early."

"Maybe I can find something for Blue," Cory said as she fell into step beside Laudine. "He's been concerned about my safety when he should be putting all his energy into studying for his test. Do you think she has candles that can help someone worry less?"

CHAPTER
15

I'm coming in with you this time," Macks said as he drove Cory and Laudine to the Little Match Girl's house the next day. "I didn't like that you went into that trade show without me. Blue would never forgive me if anything happened to you and neither would I."

"You're welcome to come if you want to, Macks," said Cory. "But I doubt it's necessary. We're just going in to meet the girl."

"I know, but . . . What the heck? What's going on here?" Macks asked as they turned onto the street where the Match Girl lived.

The street was lined with little bungalows, not at all the kind of place that normally drew a crowd, but a large group of people was gathered in front of one house, shouting and shaking placards.

"That's her house, isn't it?" Cory said.

Laudine nodded. "It's the right address. Look at the signs those people are waving. I don't think they're happy with her work."

Cory peered out the window to read the signs.

LITTLE MATCH GIRL IS BURNED OUT!

OUR LOVE WENT UP IN SMOKE!

"I'm definitely going in with you," Macks said as he parked the car.

After opening the car doors for Cory and Laudine, Macks led the way through the crowd. People glared at him as he pushed past, but no one seemed eager to confront an ogre.

"If you're looking for love, don't ask her for help," a woman called to Cory. "She conned us and won't give our money back!"

"We want our money!" another woman screamed at the house. "You're a crook! The love didn't last!"

Macks stepped onto the porch and knocked. When no one answered, he began to pound on the door so hard that it looked as if he was about to break it down.

The door opened a crack and a young woman peeked out. "I'm not giving any refunds. It said so in the contract. And the guarantee only said that you'd fall in love, not that you'd stay in love."

"I don't want a refund," Laudine said, stepping onto the porch. "I just want to talk to you. Please let me in."

"Why should I?" the girl said, but her eyes grew wide when she saw Laudine. "Miss Kundry! Yes, of course!"

Laudine stepped inside when the girl opened the door wide. Before she could close it, Cory and Macks followed the president of Witches United into the house. Some of the protesters tried to come in as well, but Macks growled and shut the door in their faces.

"This is an honor, Miss Kundry!" said the girl.

Cory recognized her right away. Although she was wearing her hair differently, it was definitely the girl with the braids who had worked for the caterer at Delphinium's wedding. She had seemed confident and slightly cocky then; now she looked like a student who had just been called into the principal's office.

"What is your name, girl?" Laudine said in an authoritative voice. "Not this 'Match Girl' nonsense, but your real name."

"Janiss Hartsthorne," the girl said in a near whisper.

Laudine took a pad of leaves from her purse and flipped through it until she found the name. "I see. You're a grade-two witch, so you're little more than a beginner. You've been specializing in incantations and food preparation spells, yet now you claim to have the ability to make matches. How is that possible?"

Janiss looked around as if trying to find an escape route, but her gaze fell on Cory and her eyes lit up. "It's her fault!" she cried. "It was her music that did it!"

"What are you talking about?" asked Cory.

"I work for a caterer who handles weddings, funerals, and birthday parties. When I heard at the last minute that Zephyr was going to be playing at the goblin wedding, I grabbed a device that I'd just bought from Abracadabra Music. I recorded all the songs Zephyr played at the wedding, but the best one was the last one. When I saw what it did to people, I knew I could make money off it. Incantation classes aren't cheap and I needed help paying my bills. I thought if I called myself a matchmaker, people would come to me and I could play that song. They'd fall in love just like the people did when they heard Zephyr play. I helped my first few customers for free and they told all their friends about me. After that, I had more people than I could handle."

"Did you write the song she's talking about?" Laudine asked Cory.

"Yes, but it's just a song!" said Cory. "My mother asked me to write one for her wedding. It was never meant to make people fall in love. And I certainly didn't mean for it to be used this way!"

"You're lying!" cried Janiss. "No one can put that much power into a song without meaning to! If you came here to accuse me of using unlicensed magic, Miss Kundry, I'm not the one you should go after. She is! She's the one who wrote it!"

"Perhaps," said Laudine. "But intent is everything in a case like this. Hold out your right hand."

Janiss raised her hand and hesitated. Laudine gestured and Janiss's hand shot out, palm up. The girl gasped and tried to pull her hand back, but all she could do was make it quiver. Laudine reached into her purse and took out a round object with her seal printed on one side. Pressing the seal to the girl's palm, she left a glowing imprint that quickly faded.

"What did you just do?" Cory asked.

"I placed a warrant on her," Laudine replied. "Now she has to appear at the next meeting of the Witches United board for judgment and sentencing. She'll go whether she wants to or not—she won't be able to help it."

"What about all those people outside my house?" asked Janiss.

"That's a problem that you created and will have to deal with yourself," Laudine told her. "Perhaps next time you'll think before you try another business venture like this."

Macks led the way out of the house. As soon as Cory and Laudine followed him through the door, Janiss slammed it behind them. They had almost reached the solar car when Cory had a vision. She froze in place while Macks opened the car door. When she didn't get in, Laudine asked, "Is something wrong?"

The first face Cory *saw* was Janiss's. When another face formed beside it, Cory gasped. The other person in her vision was Perky.

"No, nothing's wrong," Cory said as the vision faded. This time she knew both of the people. She even knew where to find them. As far as Cory was concerned, the only problem with matching Janiss to Perky was that she wasn't sure she liked the match.

They were on their way home when Laudine placed another privacy bubble around them. Turning to Cory, she said, "I didn't know your songs were so powerful."

Cory sighed. "I didn't either until I saw how people reacted to my song 'Lily Rose.' I'm the only person who didn't cry when Zephyr played it. I wrote the love song later only because my mother asked me to. I never intended to make people fall in love because of it, though. You can't imagine how surprised I was when Janiss said that she'd used a recording of the song to make people fall in love. The people who heard Zephyr play in person may stay in love a little longer, but I doubt very much that it will be permanent. It's not like I shot them with my arrows. Tell me something. What's going to happen to that girl, Janiss?"

"That depends on what the board decides," Laudine told her. "She could be suspended from using magic for as little as a week to as much as a year. She'll be better off facing the board than if I had judged her. I'm probably stricter than most. I've always felt that any misuse of magic is a crime that should be severely punished."

Macks was parking in front of the house when three women got out of a car that was parked on the street. As the women started walking up the drive, all three were watching Laudine. Cory was dismayed to see that one of the women was Hagatha Smerch.

"We need to talk to you, Laudine," called Hagatha. "Let's go in your house so we can have some privacy."

"We can talk out here," said Laudine.

"Then send your friend and the ogre away."

"No," Laudine told her. "I won't. They are both welcome to stay. What do you want, Hagatha?"

"I've talked to the members of the board, and they're ready to decree that all matchmakers are phony and guilty of public deception. This includes your little friend Cory."

Hagatha gave Cory a disdainful look. The other two women just looked disgusted.

"That may be true of the one who has called herself the 'Little Match Girl,' but I don't agree that what you say is true of them all."

"We know you went to see Janiss Hartsthorne and are sending her to the board, but why didn't you do the same with your friend Cory? She made matches and was paid very well for them, from what we hear."

"Because she is a true matchmaker and did not deceive anyone," Laudine said, staring the other women down. "Anyone who claims otherwise is deluding herself."

"Think what you will," said Hagatha. "But we believe that you may have been bought off. If that is not the case, then you are simply getting old and making bad decisions. Either way, you are no longer worthy of being the president of Witches United."

"Don't forget the trade show," said one of the other women.

"Ah, yes," Hagatha continued. "We found it most disturbing that you brought an outsider to one of our trade shows, exposing her to our secrets that are for witches' eyes only. The board will most definitely hear about this as well."

"Go right ahead, tell them," Laudine replied. "I haven't done anything wrong."

CHAPTER
16

The next day, Cory was in her office, thumbing through yearbooks, when Macks barged in. "I was in the front yard with Shimmer, and a bunch of witches showed up. One of them knocked on Laudine's door. When she came out, they put some sort of spell on her so she couldn't move and stuck her in a car. I heard them talking. They're taking her to WU headquarters for an inquisition."

"I don't know what a witches' inquisition is, but it sounds really bad," Cory said as she pushed her chair back.

Lionel stepped into the room behind the ogre. "Is something wrong?" he asked Macks. "I heard you running down the hall."

"Some witches just took Laudine to the WU head-quarters for an inquisition," Cory told him. "A witch named Hagatha was accusing her of all sorts of things yesterday, and she kept bringing up my name. I think that helping me is what got Laudine in trouble. I need to go see if I can help her."

"I've heard about those inquisitions, and they can be quite nasty," Lionel told them. "I'll go with you. Blue took the day off to study, but I think he'll want to go as well. Witches holding an inquisition can be capable of anything. It wouldn't hurt to have a FLEA officer along."

"If we're going to face a bunch of riled-up witches, I think Cran and Andrue should go, too. I'll tell them what's going on and get the car started," Macks said, and hurried from the room.

"I hope Laudine is all right," said Cory. "I'll feel awful if anything happens to her. I made her vow that she wouldn't tell anyone about me. I don't think she'll even be able to say my name when they question her."

"If they do anything to Laudine because she helped a Cupid, they'll have to deal with me," said Lionel.

"And me!" Cory said, her fingers curling into fists.

Blue and the three ogres were already waiting outside when Cory and her grandfather left the house. They all piled into the car, leaving Shimmer whimpering as she peered out a downstairs window. Macks drove while Lionel and Blue gave him directions. They sped through town, avoiding the busier streets, and arrived in front of the headquarters with screeching brakes.

It was a lovely stone building with large windows set well back from the street. Trees and flowers edged the walk that led to the front door, making it look very inviting. As Cory and her grandfather started up the walk, Blue and the ogres hurried to flank them as if they were expecting trouble. They didn't see anyone, however, until they entered the front lobby. It was a large, bright room with a stone floor and a high, vaulted ceiling decorated with shining stars. The only furniture in it were a big desk and a few uncomfortable-looking chairs. A young woman seated at the desk looked up and said, "May I help you?"

"We're here for the inquisition," Lionel told her.

"May I see your identification?" the witch asked.

Blue reached into his pocket and pulled out his FLEA badge. "Where is the inquisition being held?"

"I meant your witch ID," said the young woman.

"We're not witches," Cory told her.

The witch picked up a wand that was lying on her desk. "Then I'm afraid I can't let you in. You all have to leave or I'll be forced to call security."

Lionel held up his hand. "Do not push me, little girl," he said as his hand started to glow.

The witch pressed a button on the desk and a panel slid back in the ceiling. With a loud squawk, two gargoyles dropped through the opening. The girl pointed the wand at the group and said, "Get them out of here."

The gargoyles were swooping down with their claws out and their wings tucked back when Lionel's hand became so bright that everyone had to look away. "Leave us alone and go back where you came from," he said in a voice that had its own echo.

The gargoyles screeched and pulled up short. When they started to circle above him, Lionel raised his hand and the glow pulsed like a steady heartbeat. The pulse slammed into the gargoyles as if it were a tangible thing, hurling them back. They hit the ceiling, cracking it. Most of the stars went out. The air knocked out of them, the gargoyles fell, spreading their wings again just before they hit the floor. Shrieking, they flew back to the open panel in the ceiling and clawed their way inside.

Macks roared and slammed his fist on the desk, breaking it in two. "I'll wreck this place if I have to," he growled. "Stop wasting our time. Where is the inquisition?"

The young woman sat frozen, staring at Lionel.

"Don't bother," said Blue. "She looked in this direction when I asked where it was being held. It's through this door."

"That thing you did with your hand was amazing," Cory told her grandfather as they followed Blue. "Can I do that?"

He smiled and nodded. "You can. You've only just begun to learn everything that you can do."

"Then I want to learn that hand thing next," Cory said. "Can you teach it to me tomorrow?"

Lionel laughed. "I'll teach you whatever you want to know, but a lot of it will just come to you when you need it."

Blue opened the door and peered inside. "Would you look at this!" he said.

The room beyond was much bigger than the foyer. It had a low ceiling and was poorly lit and gloomy. The stone floor felt damp underfoot, and the air was cold and musty as if they were entering a long-abandoned basement. Chains hung from the walls and there were grooves in the floor. Cory didn't want to think about what they might be for.

"Is this a dungeon or what?" Cran muttered. "It looks like a room my grandfather had in his house. We used to play there when we were kids. My mother hated that room. She didn't like anything that was so old-fashioned."

"Shh!" Andrue whispered. "Listen!"

Cory could hear it then, a soft sound as if hundreds of voices were chanting. She turned her head, trying to locate the origin of the sound, but it seemed to be coming from everywhere.

Her grandfather touched her arm and pointed. "Over there," he said.

One end of the room seemed to be filled with shadows. Cory and Lionel started walking in that direction, moving as quietly as they could. Once again Blue and the ogres split up to walk on either side. As they drew closer, Cory could see that the shadows were actually people wearing long robes with cowls covering their heads, standing in a circle. Cory thought they were chanting in some arcane language, but when she listened carefully she realized that they were just holding whispered conversations.

"Did you see Morticia's hair lately? It looks as if she's going bald."

"I need to go grocery shopping. I hope the store is still open when we get out of here."

"I think I'm catching a cold. I've had the sniffles all day."

"How long do we have to wait for her? I have a date tonight."

When Cory was close enough, she could see that the only person wearing ordinary clothes was a woman standing in the middle with her head hanging. It looked as if something invisible was holding her up. Suddenly, she stirred and raised her head. It was Laudine.

"She woke up," one of the robed people said.

"It's about time," someone else declared. "This robe itches. When was the last time these things were washed?"

"Hagatha, you called for this inquisition," said a high-pitched, nasal voice. "Step forward and state your case for all to hear."

"Excuse me. Pardon me. Coming through," Hagatha said as she made her way to the front. Laudine glared when the other witch came to stand in the circle. Ignoring her, Hagatha pushed her cowl off her head and looked around at the others. "As you all know, I was appointed to investigate Laudine Kundry's fitness to continue on as our president. After a thorough examination of the facts, I deem her unfit and unworthy."

"That's no surprise!" someone standing near Cory whispered to the person beside her. "She got all her friends to 'appoint' her. Most of them didn't even know what they were appointing her for."

"What evidence do you have?" asked the nasal voice. Cory's eyes were adjusting to the dim light, and she could finally make out the little woman who was talking.

"One of the president's duties is to look into the unauthorized or unlicensed use of magic. I maintain that Laudine Kundry has been remiss in her duties, specifically with regard to one Corialis Feathering. This young woman is known to have made money by offering her services as a matchmaker. I studied the records and found that she is not a witch and that she never, at any time, applied for or received permission to use love potions or any other magic related to love. Although none of her old clients were available to testify against her, I have found a new client who was able to record such a transaction."

"That isn't possible," Cory whispered to her grandfather. "I haven't taken on any new clients lately."

"Poppy Thistlethwaite, please step forward," said Hagatha.

A figure slipped through the crowd and went to stand beside Hagatha. "Cory Feathering is a phony. I paid her good money and she promised she would make a match for me. But she didn't. I still haven't met my true love."

Cory leaned toward her grandfather and whispered in his ear. "It's all a lie. I can't let her get away with this."

"Let her finish first," he whispered back.

"Do you have proof that you hired her?" asked Hagatha.

"I do," said Poppy. She tried to stick her hand in her pocket, but the robe she was wearing got in the way. After fumbling around for a minute, she finally pulled the robe off over her head and dropped it on the floor.

"I'm taking mine off, too," said the witch standing near Cory. "This robe is making me sweat! I don't know why we have to wear these things."

Cory moved out of the way as the witch pulled off her robe and bunched it into a ball, dropping it on the floor beside her purse. Now Cory could see that the witch was an older woman who was probably close to Laudine's age. Taking their cue from her, a number of other witches removed their robes as well.

With her robe off, Poppy was able to reach into her pocket and take out a shiny black cube. Setting it on the floor, she pushed the top and stepped back. An image appeared, only slightly brighter than the room, and it wasn't very good. Cory squinted and was able to make out the image of someone who resembled her, talking to someone who looked like Poppy.

"I've heard rumors that you're a matchmaker," said the image of Poppy. "Is it true?"

"Yes, it is," said the image that looked something like Cory.

"If I paid you, would you make a match for me?" asked Poppy's image.

The image that looked like Cory nodded. "Yes, as long as you pay me enough money."

"Here," said Poppy's image. "Here is the money you require."

"Then I will find you your one true love," the Cory-like image said as it took the money.

"That so never happened!" Cory whispered to Lionel. "And you know I don't talk like that!"

"Then you need to tell them that it's a lie," said her grandfather.

"Excuse me," Cory said, slipping between the witches in front of her. "I have something to say!"

"You see!" Hagatha declared as Poppy turned off the black device. "Cory Feathering did engage in an unlawful and unsanctioned transaction."

"I did not!" Cory announced, reaching the middle of the circle. "I'm Cory Feathering. Everything Poppy just told you and everything on that recording is a lie!"

"I am not a liar!" Poppy declared. "All of that actually happened!"

"Maybe people actually said those things, but I was not the person who looked like me! I bet you got one of your friends to do it. Or maybe you hired someone, but

I never said any of that. When exactly was this supposed to have happened?"

"I don't remember," said Poppy.

One of the witches raised her hand in the air. "I have one of those recorders. The date you make the recording shows up on the top when you play it."

"I'll look," said the witch with the high-pitched voice. "I see the date. It was seven days ago."

"Seven days ago I was in a goblin warren getting ready for my mother's wedding," Cory told them. "You can ask any of the goblins who were there with me."

The witches stirred as they looked from Cory to Poppy to Hagatha.

"I can settle this," said the older witch who had been standing near Cory. She bent down to pick up something, then marched to the middle of the circle. Muttering to herself, she reached into her purse and took out a crystal ball. She was holding it with one hand when she took out a small white object and plugged it into the side of the ball. "Let's see if this amplifier actually works. It had better. I paid enough for it."

The witches near her stepped back as the older witch murmured something. A moment later a fuzzy image appeared in the ball, while a larger, projected image appeared on the ceiling.

As the image came into focus, Cory could see herself holding Shimmer. Poppy was there, eyeing the little dragon. "Tell me something," said Poppy. "I've heard rumors that you're a matchmaker. Is it true?"

"I have helped some of my friends make matches in the past," Cory told her.

"If I paid you, would you make a match for me?" asked Poppy.

Cory shook her head. "I'm not doing that anymore."

The image faded, then came back a moment later. This time, they were wearing different clothes and Cory wasn't holding Shimmer.

"Word is going around that someone calling herself the 'Little Match Girl' is making matches between couples and the matches really work," said Poppy. "She does it with one date and they fall in love every time. If I were looking for a match, should I go to her or you?"

"I don't know this person, so I have no idea what her abilities might be, but I'm not taking on clients for money anymore," said Cory. "I really can't help you."

"I can pay you whatever you're asking," Poppy told her.

"Sorry, but it isn't a matter of payment," Cory said.

"Uh-huh," said Poppy. "I get it. You only help your friends!"

The image was fading when Hagatha started talking again. "The only thing those images prove is that Poppy Thistlethwaite was not a client of Cory Feathering. However, Cory herself admits that she made matches in the past for money."

"That's true," said Cory.

"And do you currently make matches for people?" Hagatha asked her.

"I do," Cory replied. "But not for money."

"There you have it! Perhaps she didn't help Poppy, but she is a self-proclaimed matchmaker! I maintain that her neighbor Laudine Kundry knew about this. When I questioned her weeks ago, asking if she had looked into Cory Feathering, she said that she had and that Cory was not breaking any rules. Now that we know Cory was indeed breaking the rules, we also know that Laudine was either inept, a poor judge of the situation, or that Cory Feathering bought her off. Laudine even took Miss Feathering to the witches' trade show, which she knows full well only witches may attend. Whatever the reason, I say that Laudine Kundry should be stripped of her rights as president of Witches United. According to our rule book, she should be impeached as president, suspended from witchhood, lose her *WU Today* subscription, be expelled from the witches' country club,

and be subject to eternal torture, the type to be deter-
mined at some future date."

Laudine tried to speak, but when her lips moved,
nothing came out.

Cory glanced at her grandfather and mouthed the
words, "I'm sorry. I have to do this."

Lionel nodded and mouthed, "I know. It's all right."

Cory took a step forward and said, "Laudine Kundry
is not guilty of any of the things you've accused her of
doing. She did investigate me, but when she learned the
truth, I made her take a vow that she would never reveal
my secret."

"Why would she agree to that?" demanded Hagatha.

"Because of what I am," said Cory. Closing her eyes,
she thought, *Wings!* They were there an instant later,
glowing and iridescent. Every witch in the room
gasped.

Cory thought about love then. She thought about
Blue and how happy she felt when he was around. She
thought about the pride that had shown on his face
when she played "Lily Rose" at the Battle of the Bands.
She remembered how much fun it had been to run the
obstacle course together. And she remembered the joy
on Quince's and Micah's faces when the judge pro-
nounced them man and wife, and the way Wilburton
Deeds looked whenever he was near Delphinium.

Even before Cory opened her eyes, the rosy glow behind her eyelids told her that she had banished the dark. When she looked around, she saw that her glow had reached to every corner of the room, even erasing the shadows. It was only when she looked down that she realized she was suspended six feet above the floor, and that she was holding her bow in one hand and her quiver in the other. The witches were silent as they gazed up at her with their mouths open. She almost laughed when she saw the awed expressions on the ogres' faces. Although Lionel looked both pleased and proud, the only thing she saw on Blue's face was love. It was more than enough.

"I am Corialis Feathering and I am Cupid!" she said in a voice that didn't sound quite like her own. "Your rules and regulations about love do not apply to me!"

"She's a demigod!" one of the witches cried; the words were taken up all around the room.

Cory turned to Laudine and their eyes met. "I release you from your solemn promise," she told her friend.

The glow that surrounded Cory suddenly grew brighter. Laudine staggered and her hair blew back from her face as if wind had touched her for an instant. As Cory settled to the floor, the rosy glow faded, but the room still didn't seem nearly as dark as before.

"I declare that Laudine Kundry is innocent of all charges," the older witch announced. "She is still our president and I hope will continue to be for a very long time!"

"I love your wings and your bow!" a young witch gushed.

Cory glanced behind her. "Oh, I forgot," she said, and thought, *Wings! Bow!*

Her wings, bow, and quiver all disappeared in an instant, making the witches around her gasp.

"Thank you so much, Cory!" said Laudine. "I couldn't refute anything because I couldn't tell them about you."

"I know, and I'm sorry that I put you in that position," Cory told her.

"And I'm sorry you had to tell them your secret," said Laudine. "I hope it doesn't make things harder for you."

"I don't know what's going to happen," Cory confessed, but even as she said it, a vision started to form. To her surprise, she *saw* Daisy and a slightly older man in a strange uniform. Perhaps she did know what was going to happen after all.